Dear [ ],

May God richly bless you & protect you. I hope this little novel places a unique message in your heart.

Love & Prayers,
[signature]
05-21-12

Fingernail Moon

J. Laura Chandler

CROSSBOOKS

CrossBooks™
A Division of LifeWay
1663 Liberty Drive
Bloomington, IN 47403
www.crossbooks.com
Phone: 1-866-879-0502

©2011 J. Laura Chandler. All rights reserved.

No part of this book may be reproduced, stored in a retrieval system, or transmitted by any means without the written permission of the author.

First published by CrossBooks 09/20/2011

ISBN: 978-1-6150-7812-7 (sc)
ISBN: 978-1-4627-0082-0 (e)

Scripture taken from the New King James Version. Copyright 1979, 1980, 1982 by Thomas Nelson, inc. Used by permission. All rights reserved.

Printed in the United States of America

This book is printed on acid-free paper.

Any people depicted in stock imagery provided by Thinkstock are models, and such images are being used for illustrative purposes only.

Certain stock imagery © Thinkstock.

Because of the dynamic nature of the Internet, any web addresses or links contained in this book may have changed since publication and may no longer be valid. The views expressed in this work are solely those of the author and do not necessarily reflect the views of the publisher, and the publisher hereby disclaims any responsibility for them.

Dedication

This book is dedicated to the memory of my loving parents . . . .
I continue to learn from you.

Acknowledgements

My children who believed in their mother and cheered me on to complete and publish *Fingernail Moon*. My husband, Rich, who patiently listened and believed in me to the final page. And special thanks to my dear friends Deanna Stanley and Dianne Anderson for graciously editing *Fingernail Moon*.

2007

I'm not sure what part gripped my heart so strongly . . . . the way he carried himself, the platinum hair sparkling in the afternoon sun rays, or just his sheer innocence. Whatever it was though changed both of our lives forever!

Now, some twenty years later, I have learned that God always had my heart in his hands, and by His never-failing providence is in control of every event and brings good from evil, but, I still find myself both physically and emotionally imprisoned in my present valley. *Oh, Lord in Heaven give us a mountain top as high as this valley is deep. I am in utter distress, and I covet Your presence, sweet Jesus.*

1987

Sunday afternoons seemed to serve only as a spring board for what Monday mornings at work would lash out. It had been a grueling week, and right now was just not the time for listening to colleagues drone on about their weekend activities, so why not a peaceful stroll in the wooded park on the north side of town. There were nature trails, fountains and the crisp air would be the perfect atmosphere for relaxing and observing people. The temperatures were uncharacteristically cool, so this was the perfect day to take a walk in the park. Belle had always enjoyed "people watching." As she parked her car, she glimpsed a movement by the passenger's side. It was a very small boy, not much more than three or four years old. She looked around to see where his parents were or the person supervising, but saw no one. She decided to keep her eye on the little fellow, at least until he was safely under supervision. Her mind wandered to the many children she had encountered under the authority of the State Welfare Department. Thankfully, though, her firm had been able to find homes for a few children who were previously neglected and abused. Some of the older children, not as fortunate as the younger ones, were constantly relocated from one foster home to another. Her firm screened prospective adoptive parents for the Welfare Department, and she had seen firsthand how difficult some of the adjustments were for children. Suddenly, she realized she had walked at least a half mile when she again observed the little boy was unsupervised. Finally, he ran up to a young woman who was stretched out on a bench. He took her hand and tugged on her, "Mom . . . " But she shouted at him and waved him away. He was the most beautiful little boy Belle had ever seen. Oh, how her heart ached for this precious child.

She thought. "Why do people have children when they really do not want them?"

As Belle observed the mother and son, she noticed that he was not given a chance to express what was on his mind. This really bothered her. She began to think about what this little boy's life could be like with the proper guidance, encouragement and loving kindness. Belle sat down on a bench several yards from them, pondering how unfair it seemed for such an innocent child to be so uncared for. Finally, the woman jerked her little boy up from where he was seated playing with his little car in the dirt. "We're going home, now."

Belle slowly walked to her car which was parked several spaces over from the woman's vehicle. She wondered how in the world she could be thinking of following these strangers, but follow she did. They had not traveled far before the woman turned to enter a relatively nice neighborhood. Taking a right turn on the second street over, which Belle noted as Bellvue, the woman turned into the seventh driveway on the right. Belle saw no other car parked in the driveway, and surmised this may be a single parent and child.

At home that night Belle simply could not get her mind off the little boy. Was he happy? Certainly, it did not appear so. Was his mother good to him? What she witnessed didn't give her a good comfort level. She just had a gut feeling all was not right with the lad.

Be patient, Belle. Just enjoy this wonderful cup of coffee and go with the flow. The traffic was bottlenecked for no apparent reason, and she could think of a dozen or more documents on her desk that needed to be signed. Monday morning—she could already hear the reflective chatter of all those domestic weekends. Sometimes all the family talk irritated her, and other times it saddened her.

She had carved out a perfect little niche in the singles world. And single was true in every way. Her parents were dead. They had adopted her in their latter years. Her mom did have a younger sister who was still alive, but the vast distance in miles between them had given Belle an excuse to be remiss in communicating and staying in touch, and she had only a vague recollection of grandparents, since both sets died when she was very young.

Was she happy? Too busy to analyze! Her career was extremely gratifying. After working hard to get a degree in psychology, she had a total change of heart and prolonged the agony of two more years of school to become a paralegal. The firm she worked for was demanding, but she had to admit, the challenges were stimulating. They couldn't do without her.

As she entered the office, Sissy rolled her eyes and looked over toward the couple waiting in the reception office. "Ms. Hamilton, the couple in the waiting room had an 8:30 appointment with you, and you'll never believe it; there last name is the same as yours! Shall I escort them into the conference area?"

"Yes, I'll be in shortly."

Quickly she walked to her office, signed off on several urgent documents, handed several organized stacks of paper to Sissy for processing, and picked up the Hamilton file. What are the chances of meeting someone here at the office with the same last name as hers? Maybe an omen of some kind. You just never know!

As she approached the conference room she could hear the couple telling each other what to say, and what not to say! "Good morning, Mr. & Mrs. Hamilton. Seems we all have the same last name here! My name is Belle Hamilton and you may just call me Belle. Sorry I'm running late this morning, but we'll jump right to the heart of the matter, and not waste any more of your valuable time. I understand that you want to adopt a child through our firm."

"Yes, Ms. Hamilton!"

"It's okay to just call me Belle. May be less confusing. Mr. Hamilton, are you and your wife in total agreement regarding the decision to adopt?"

"Well, I'm just fine like we are with no children, but Sylvia feels like her life will not be complete without a child, so I'm in agreement with her desire to adopt."

"Folks, you realize that our firm interviews many couples whenever we have one child that can possibly be adopted. We try to insure that both parents not only accept all the responsibilities that rearing a child entails, but that both parties want to make a major contribution in this child's life. This commitment is one that both parents truly have to want individually, as well as jointly."

"Ms. Hamilton, I intend to honor this commitment for the sake of my wife."

"I see," Belle spoke softly. "Well," trying to sound upbeat, "This is just one of several interviews, and I know you two have documentation on all the fees involved in an adoption through our firm. Let me suggest that you review your financial obligations, not only our fees, but the expenses which are outlined for the child's welfare, education, and so forth. We will schedule another time for the two of you to come back in for further evaluation."

"Ms. Hamilton, I hope you know how much I need a child," pleaded the wife.

"Mrs. Hamilton, I assure you, that on a personal level as a woman, I know the desire in your heart to have a child, and we really do want what is best for you and the child. I'm sure everything will work out just fine. If you will, please stop by our front desk and have my assistant, Sissy, set you up for another appointment, and we'll see you then."

As the couple meandered down the hall, Belle thought about how many couples she had interviewed over the past six years. All of them wanted to adopt children, but aside from that, they were all so different. Thank goodness, Belle was not the only one making a decision on which couples were appropriate adoptive parents. She worked with Jeff Starnes, one of the senior partners. Mr. Starnes had placed total confidence in Belle's ability to initially screen all candidates, and she took pride in that. So much so, that she herself believed she would be the perfect mother. She would one day nurture and care for her child like no other before her.

"One day," she thought with a sigh. "Maybe one day."

John Marshall, his head in his hands, pondered the previous day's events. He and his wife, Kate, had a horrible fight which was witnessed by their son, Eddie. Kate had pulled Eddie into the car and sped out of the driveway before John could even think about how to respond. Indifference and contention had become a way of life for their little family, and seemed to disrupt every good plan or intention he had.

"Oh Kate," John mumbled, "where did I go wrong?"

After completing law school, John had made a pact with God, that he would be head of household, and lead his family down the straight and narrow way, if only God would bring the right woman into his life.

Kate was everything John could have ever hoped for, but probably not the wife who God had in mind. She had a beautiful figure, that all American smile, loved a challenge, and didn't mind risks. When they had talked about getting married with the prospect of starting his own practice, Kate seemed to welcome the challenges of a new law practice.

John thought, "I've got to find a way to make it better for Eddie. I'm always under a cloud of guilt when I do the least bit of reflecting concerning our boy. I can't seem to focus on his needs because of being consumed with Kate's behavior."

Kate had only one minor flaw when John met her. She smoked marijuana! John felt that after settling down into married life, the pot would lose its appeal. And then Eddie was born and Kate's postpartum depression never left. Now, she was smoking pot, drinking, and perhaps hiding some other addiction as well.

"What's that verse in the Bible about being equally yoked? Look how far off track I've gotten from God's Word." John moaned.

Oh God, I'm such a coward; please bring about a change in our lives.

Picking up the phone, he gave Kate a call. "Hi there, how's your day going?"

"It's going," Kate slurred.

"How's Eddie doing?"

"I guess he's okay—the little roamer. He'd rather be visiting with all the neighbors than playing in his own yard."

"Why don't you take him to the park? Just you and him—quality time away from the TV and telephone. What do you think?"

Kate shot back, "Why don't you take him to the park? Just you and him—quality time away from the TV and telephone. I think that's a father and son thing, growled Kate. Anyway, you don't know how I feel. I don't have all the energy you have. By the way, why don't you pick up something for supper tonight?"

"Fine Kate, whatever . . . honey, I love yo . . . " Click.

"That was my husband," Kate said. "Yeah, yeah . . . . I'm good for it. You know I am. He is so consumed with his law practice, he rarely questions anything regarding our finances. Just hurry up and bring the stuff over here."

"I'll have to talk with my boss, but I'm sure things can be worked out, Mrs. Marshall." Albert said.

―

If Belle had thought about the little boy once, she must have thought about him a hundred times throughout the morning. No harm in taking a ride by his house during lunch. She needed a break from the office anyway. The more she thought about it the more excited she became.

The last prospective adoptive parents left, and Belle was out the door, heart pumping hard, and again feeling like an intruder trespassing into a stranger's personal life.

Before Belle turned onto the boy's street, she saw the little tow head riding his tricycle. He was at least two blocks from his house. She slowed the car and smiled at him. He immediately started chatting about his dog . . . had she seen him? His speech was so clear to be as young as he was. She asked him his name. He replied, "My name is Eddie, and my dog is Barney. I have to find Barney."

Belle mused, "His name is Eddie. Funny, he doesn't look like an Eddie."

"I tell you what, Eddie, if you'll tell me what Barney looks like, I'll drive on up this street, and see if I can find him, okay?"

Before Belle could get a reply, the little fellow was pedaling hard going even farther from his house. She couldn't imagine a three year or four year old being out of his own yard without adult supervision.

Hurriedly Belle drove back to the office, too preoccupied with little Eddie to stop for lunch. The afternoon flew by. Most of the office personnel had left for the day, and Belle just sat at her desk in deep thought about this little boy who had such a grip on her heart.

—

John turned the corner toward his house with the same cloud of dread which engulfed him every day upon returning from work. Why did he set himself up for disappointment? The scene, the routine, the conversation and the unkempt house, which was fast becoming filthy, greeted him night after night. Always, he hoped that things would miraculously change.

Eddie greeted him with tears and hope. "Dad, I've been looking for Barney all day. Would you please find him for me? Mom can't help, but I know Barney will come to you."

John's heart sank at the prospect of one more emotional trauma piled on top of Mount Everest. "I tell you what, Eddie, let's eat our supper while it is still warm, and then we'll take a ride around the neighborhood and see if we can locate Barney."

Eddie seemed mildly soothed, and promptly walked over to the table and sat down.

"Kate, I'm home, let's eat!"

John set the table, and served the Chinese cuisine he had picked up in town.

Kate dragged herself to the table, and proceeded to pick at her food.

"No appetite tonight?" John commented.

"John, don't start in on me as soon as you get in!"

Eating in silence, John tried to remember when times were different. Coming home every night was his worst nightmare. Their home was only a house. The only spark of life was Eddie. Everything else was only a numb existence. Eddie sometimes wore the same dirty clothes from one day to the next, and this ripped at John's heart. Hired help was desperately needed, but no one would stay more than a couple of days, and then you never heard from them again.

Kate needed to be institutionalized until the drugs were out of her system, and then outpatient treatment would probably be needed for a while afterwards. He had broached the subject several times, and she had become so irate that she threatened to take Eddie and leave without a trace!

Kate looked ten years older than her age. She was so thin, and had the look of a boy rather than the voluptuous young woman he had married. Something had to be done! Tomorrow . . . .

"Okay, Eddie. Let's jump in the car and go find Barney."

Eddie ran to the door, full of hope and said, "Dad, I just know you can do it!" Instead of this making John feel confident, it just seemed to pierce his heart deeper. He had let his whole family down. Failure loomed over him bigger than day. *Dear Lord, please let us find our dog.*

They drove throughout the whole neighborhood without a sign of Barney. John had stopped and asked several people if they had seen the little Sheltie, but no one had seen the dog.

John decided to cross the highway and explore a newly developed subdivision. Just a hunch. Sure enough, he spied Barney on the front porch of a newly constructed house. Someone had fed him, and he looked to be enjoying his supper to the fullest!

Eddie spotted Barney immediately, too. "Dad, there he is. Oh, Dad, I'm so happy!"

Eddie called his pup and Barney leaped into the car. John breathed a sigh of relief. *Thank you, Lord. This is my spark of happiness.*

—

Belle awoke with her heart pounding like the hooves of wild horses. She tried to quiet her spirit by telling herself it was only a dream. Still, her heart was in her throat. It was only a dream. No, it was a horrible nightmare. She tried to recall the details. Little Eddie was crying and being torn away from a scene involving a young woman. His clothes were stained with blood, and he seemed so pitiful and confused.

Belle decided to make some coffee, read her Bible, and await the rising sun in the great room. "I couldn't sleep if I wanted to," she thought. "I am very definitely disturbed over this whole situation." After looking up a few scriptures on dreams and visions, the thought occurred to Belle that she could have had some kind of vision, couldn't she? What could she do about any of this? It was none of her business. Why was she so plagued by this whole thing? Oh, the battles that go on in one's head. Okay, okay. What is to be, is to be!

She read until she dozed off in the recliner.

—

Albert was having one of his panic attacks. Where was the valium? He worked for a drug dealer, and couldn't even find one valium when he needed it.

The confrontation Albert had with Guy earlier was making him feel weak and queasy. Where was that confidence level he had maintained for the last year or so? There was no reason to be scared. He could bully his way with this dame. However, she posed a real threat to his so far flawless career running drugs for Guy. It had been easy street up until now, and the pay was excellent, too.

Guy had been very explicit regarding the quantity of goods distributed to one party. He always cautioned how too much greed could backfire. But Albert had talked Guy into selling Kate a large supply because business had been a little slow, plus some customers were getting picky about the quality. Why did he sell Kate so much cocaine? She had set him up. She knew he wouldn't turn down ten grand in cash! Now, less than a month later, she wants a duplicate supply on credit. What was she doing with this amount of cocaine? Guy has a right to be steamed. Albert needed to get back to his level of comfort. Panic, and he would make big mistakes! Maybe even go to the slammer!

—

Belle was annoyed with herself for falling asleep. She had not heard the alarm clock, and it was now a quarter of nine. She picked up the phone, dialed the office, and then hung up the receiver before anyone answered.

She really needed to gather her thoughts, collect herself together and get back into the sanity zone! She picked the receiver up again, called Sissy, and told her she had some personal business to take care of today, so all appointments needed to be rescheduled accordingly. Yes, that would do! Belle had always been extremely private, and never felt she owed anyone an explanation in detail. As far as she knew, everyone had always respected her privacy. She could not remember a time that her judgment had been questioned in all the years she had worked for the firm. After all, she worked all the time and took pride in every aspect of her duties and responsibilities. She would have already been promoted to a senior partner if she had a law degree.

Belle mused, "I just want to drive by one more time and settle my mind that this kid is going to be okay." *Lord, just let me see that he is happy, and perhaps has found his little dog, Barney. I'll leave it alone for good, I promise. I'll rest in knowing that You're in control and have the plan for this precious little boy's life.*

John arrived at the office unusually early. He had left Kate sleeping on the couch with the TV going and Eddie still asleep in his bed. He prayed that Eddie would get a decent breakfast, but he doubted that it would be more than a Pop Tart or cookie.

Think, think, think . . . . what is my first step. Lord, give me the courage to take the first step, here.

John picked up the phone and made a call to a physician who a friend had recommended.

"Good morning, Dr. Garrison's office."

"Yes, this is John Marshall, and I need to talk with Dr. Garrison about my wife's mental state. I believe it is time for an intervention, and I need to know what to do first."

"Would you like to schedule an appointment? We just had a cancellation. How about 2:00 tomorrow?"

"I was hoping to get something done today," John said.

"Why don't I have Dr. Garrison give you a call later this afternoon after he has finished with patients?"

Defeated, John said, "Okay."

Belle was shaking. What in the world was she doing back in Eddie's neighborhood? Had she lost all rationale . . . . .this was none of her business. "I could get into real trouble, even trouble with the law," Belle thought. "Then why can't I turn around right now and forget all of this twisted mess in my mind?" If she saw anything at all that looked to be negligence, she would have no other choice . . . . .she would have to make this known to the proper authorities!

Turning down Eddie's street, Belle could hear clearly every beat of her heart. Her ears could hear her heart pumping as though she were listening through a stethoscope. Driving slowly and watching every movement on the street, her eye caught a glimpse of an older model car screeching out of little Eddie's driveway. Now, why would someone be speeding in this neighborhood? Slowly, she inched her way right to the edge of their property trying to look in every direction to see if anyone was watching her. Then without another thought, she turned into the driveway, slowly got out of her car, and walked in the carport. She could say that she was checking to see if their little dog, Barney, had been found. Yes, that was perfect! The door leading into the kitchen was wide open, and when she looked through the screen, she barely kept herself from screaming, but something inside her head told her to take control of herself for the boy's sake. Little Eddie was standing very still beside his mother, who was bleeding from a gaping wound in her stomach, and looked to be dead. Belle let herself in, stepped over to the boy, bent down, gathered him in her arms and asked where Barney might be. The boy jerked from her reach and ran to the back yard hollering for his little dog. Belle took a long hard look at the woman, and could see no sign of life. She opened the back door and spotted the boy and his dog. She gently guided Eddie back inside with Barney leaping and licking the little boy. Belle's head was spinning and she knew any minute she would throw up. Belle could see Eddie shaking violently. She picked him up and held him close for a moment until he calmed down. Think, Belle, think.

"Eddie, let's take Barney with us and go get help for your mom, okay?" She let him down and he slowly and obediently walked with Belle, and the three of them piled into Belle's car, and headed out of the neighborhood. She drove several miles from the area, and pulled in at a convenience store.

Belle turned to Eddie and said, "Hey, little buddy, would you and Barney wait here while I go get help?"

He nodded his little head. Belle locked the car door, quickly stepped inside and gathered sandwiches, chips, candy and drinks. She unlocked the car and handed Eddie the bag of food.

"Go ahead and eat whatever you want, and give Barney part of your sandwich, too! I'll be right back as soon as I use the phone over here."

Belle was trembling on the inside of herself and shaking on the outside. She picked up the phone with the edge of her jacket sleeve and punched in 911 with the tip of her index nail. As soon as the operator answered, she said very quickly in a disguised voice, "There's been an accident at 410 Bellvue Drive." She placed the phone back on the hook, walked straight to the car, and drove directly to her townhouse. All she could think of was protecting this innocent child.

—

John Marshall's secretary buzzed him to say a policeman needed to see him. John ended his phone call, and walked over to open his office door. "Please come in, officer. How may I help you?"

"Sir, I'm sorry to have to tell you, but your wife has been found dead."

John was certain he had heard wrong. "What did you say?" John said with a horrified look.

"Mr. Marshall, we believe your wife may have been killed."

John's only thought was Eddie. "My, son, Eddie? Where is my son, Eddie?"

"Mr. Marshall, all we've seen in your house was just the body of your wife!"

This was not happening, John was sure of it. Why, this would be his worst nightmare. It cannot be true, but the officer looked so grave.

"Oh, my God, my wife, my son, please help me," John cried and dropped to his knees.

The officer helped John to a seat on the couch and took his place across as he pulled up a chair. He could only sit motionless while John Marshall was wracked with grief and sobs.

Albert had driven back to his place. His mind was so fragmented that not one sane thought could be processed. No one would ever believe he killed in self-defense, and even if they did, who would care or give credit to a drug runner! He was toast! He showered and wrapped his flank with a torn T-shirt hoping to close off the two slashes that were oozing blood. His two worst enemies were the law and Guy. Maybe he had enough provisions to make a quick dash out of the state. Soon, he was sure, there would be a trail leading to him, especially if anyone could identify his car. He had to move quickly, but think slowly . . . . mistakes could be fatal!

—

At 410 Bellvue Drive, policemen and canines were combing the area for a little boy named Eddie Marshall. Each neighbor would be asked for their undivided assistance until Eddie could be located. Officer Nelson had questioned the neighbor who had identified Ms. Marshall, plus one other, but most had already left for work, so he was not getting much to go on. One lady at the end of the street did say the little boy was never supervised and could usually be seen anywhere in the neighborhood. The one thing that kept surfacing in Nelson's mind was drugs. It was time to have a heart to heart with the husband, secure an exact identity of his son, and have the authorities comb not only the neighborhood, but outlying areas as well.

—

Belle could feel herself getting more protective of Eddie. He had curled up in a little ball, shutting both she and Barney out of his consciousness. Belle's rationale had also taken flight. The only thing she could think of was how to protect this child from his awful past. The more she tried to convince herself to call the authorities, the more paralyzed her mind became. How could she make this right? How could she make sure Eddie would have a good life? *Oh, Lord, give this little boy a chance.* She could not bear the thought of him going back and perish the thought that this injured soul would become a part of the State Welfare system, and drift from foster home to foster home. Everything is wrong, here, and she knew that her actions were acutely wrong, but when she looked at this pure child, her heart ached, her mind was bound and all good judgment had vanished.

The only thing John could focus on was his son, Eddie. Officer Nelson had questioned him over and over about Kate, her habits, her possible connections with drugs and on and on until John thought his head and heart would explode. It was late afternoon and all he could do was walk the neighborhood calling Eddie's name. Officer Nelson had contacted his parents and Kate's to notify them of Kate's death and Eddie's disappearance. The one thing that gave John hope was the fact that Barney was also missing. Surely, the two of them just wandered off. Someone would call before long to report they had found a little boy and his dog.

Officer Nelson had spent most of the afternoon questioning John's parents about Kate's behavior. He hesitated to pry too much with Kate's folks because they were clearly devastated and in shock. Nelson was sure from the drops of blood leading out to the driveway, that whoever killed Kate was also injured. The investigative team was checking all hospitals and emergency rooms regarding anyone seen with a fresh wound. His gut feeling told him drugs had to be involved here. There would be a thorough search done throughout the house before anyone would be allowed in again. He had asked John's parents to take him to their home as it was relatively close by. He knew this would be no easy task, though. If he were John Marshall, there would be no way he would leave this area without his son.

Belle had spent much of the day in a stupor trying to make a list of needs for Eddie and Barney. Eddie and Barney were in her bed curled up together. Eddie didn't communicate. This really weighed heavily on Belle. Her compassion for this little boy had clouded discernment and good judgment on her part . . . . she knew this, and yet could not make herself call the authorities. The more she delayed, the harder it was to even think in those terms. Hadn't she started preparing to take care of Eddie herself? Of course, that was the only humane thing to do! She had called Sissy at the office and told her of Aunt Vanessa's stroke, and since she was the only family member, it was imperative that she leave right away, and she would probably return within a couple of weeks. She reminded Sissy that Aunt Vanessa had no phone, but that she would call into the office periodically.

Eddie had finally dropped off to sleep, so Belle had taken the opportunity to drive to the bank and get some cash, then run by a discount store and pick up dog food, leash, drinks, snacks, a couple of stuffed animals plus a couple of pairs of blue jeans, several shirts, pajamas and underwear for little Eddie. She had prayed the whole time she was away from Eddie that he would still be asleep when she returned, and thank the good Lord, he was! God had answered her prayer . . . . that was a good sign. Signs, signs. Funny how she had always looked for signs. The Word spoke against looking for a sign, but it always seemed to give her the affirmation she was searching for.

It was close to midnight, and Belle, Barney and Eddie were well on their way to Calveston, Texas, a little town that was situated squarely on the border of Texas and Mexico. She had been there just once not long after her parents passed away. Aunt Van's place would be a safe haven for Eddie and also give Belle time to think and sort all of this out for Eddie's best interest.

—

Albert had bound up his wounds, which were only superficial with a clean T-shirt back at the house and put close to six hundred miles between him and the horrible scene of the day. There was no way to think clearly about anything until he got some sleep, so he pulled off at a roadside park and hoped he could sleep unnoticed for a few hours.

—

John knew it would be impossible for him to sleep, and he did not understand why everyone was so insistent about it! After listening for a while to the sounds of his parents' house, he went downstairs and made a pot of coffee. There was a Bible on the sideboard in the kitchen, which beckoned John to open it. "For by grace you have been saved through faith, and that not of yourselves; it is the gift of God, not of works, lest anyone should boast." John slowly set down, and cried to God, "I am blind; I am so ignorant and lost without a prayer in this world. Oh, God, save this wretched soul and comfort me in your green pastures. I need you to carry me, Lord, as I cannot carry myself any longer. Please forgive the negligence of my own soul. Forgive me for ignoring my wife, my child, my family and most of all You, dear Lord. I need YOUR PEACE, Jesus, Your peace, You are what I need."

John's mother, Esther, tiptoed down the stairs and found her broken son asleep at the table with her Bible opened to Ephesians. Esther whispered, "Father in Heaven, give us Your Words to comfort our son, and help us to trust You with all of our hearts in all things."

Guy had not heard anything from Albert since their discussion about that crazy addict, Kate, so he decided to pick up a local paper, just to make sure there was nothing of any consequence regarding foul play. Dealing in drugs is never predictable. As he scanned the front page, he noticed the picture of a small boy. Reward offered for any information about Eddie Marshall, three and a half years old. Missing since the morning of June 2nd. Shouts were going off in Guy's head . . . . Marshall, Kate Marshall, could there be some connection? As he read further, there was his answer. Kate Marshall, mother of Eddie, was found dead on the morning of June 2nd, and authorities are almost certain, she was killed. That was enough for Guy to know that Albert's time was very short, yes he was a dead man walking right now!

Guy quickly drove to Albert's house. It was in shambles. It had been Albert's parents' old house that he inherited when his mom died. He looked around for Albert's car or evidence of someone snooping around. All was quiet, so he entered from the back, as Albert never locked the back porch door. Something told him that Albert had vacated the place and left town. Everything looked pretty normal. Guy decided to have a look around in the bathroom, and there in a trash can was part of a T-shirt with what looked to be blood smears . . . . very faint, but definitely blood. He quickly stuffed the end of it in his pocket, took another quick look around and headed out fast! Yep, he now knew Albert had left town.

The investigative team had made a thorough check of the Marshalls' house, and except for a couple of half empty wine bottles, found nothing. There was a utility shed out back which had not been searched yet, but Nelson doubted if anything would become of that. Should the autopsy on Kate reveal any evidence of drugs, then this case could very well be a murder and kidnapping. Whoever did this seemed to have vanished into thin air without a trace of evidence left behind. He needed to make sure the news media did not release any information that would prohibit his team of investigators from looking behind the scenes with regard to drug dealers and runners. The least amount of information going out to the public right now would give his team an edge.

Belle decided to stop for gas while Eddie was still sleeping. The sun would be rising soon, so she needed to fill up while things were quiet. Barney was stirring in the back seat, so she clipped the leash on so he could relieve himself. He was a great little dog, and a comfort to Belle. Funny how animals sensed an anxious spirit in someone. Barney's eyes were so trusting and he had not left Eddie's side since Belle placed them both in her car at Eddie's house. Belle still had no idea what to tell Aunt Van. She did not even know if her Aunt still lived in the same place. She remembered when Uncle Ben had died, the place was too much maintenance for any woman to keep up, and so Aunt Van could have sold the place, and moved to a smaller more manageable place in town. One thing for sure, Belle was in too deep to go back now. *Dear Lord in Heaven, help me make some sense of all of this, and please understand my deep compassion for this little boy. I ask that you give us a safe haven, dear Jesus, until we can sort this out. Lord, I ask that You have mercy on my soul for disregarding man's law. I know I am in the wrong, Father, but I cannot turn back. Please forgive me.*

—

Albert had driven as far as he could on two tanks of gas. He knew when he filled up earlier, there was a grave risk that someone would remember seeing him or identify his car. He wasn't nearly as worried about the authorities as he was Guy. He knew Guy would come in search of him. It was only a matter of time. Taking a more remote country highway, Albert decided to look for a place where he might hide his car. That was the only plan for the moment. A couple of miles past a small community, he took a left onto a gravel road. He noticed small houses spaced perhaps a quarter of a mile apart. Most places looked in need of repair and most of the yards were grown up. He crossed a rather broken down little bridge, continued on another half mile, and noticed an old woman rocking on her front porch. He drove by slowly, went on down the road until it came to a dead end, then turned around and drove back to the old woman's place. Albert pulled up into the grass-covered driveway and parked beside the house on the far side where anyone coming from the main road would more than likely not see his vehicle. He slowly stepped out and walked to the front porch.

"Mister, do I know you?"

"No ma'am, you don't. My name is Al, and I'm looking for some part-time work. Looks like you could use a handyman."

"Don't have the money, Sonny."

"That's okay, I could work for food and shelter."

"What brings you to these parts, Sonny? We don't get much traffic, especially folks we don't know."

"Ma'am, I didn't catch your name."

"You can call me Mayme. That's what all my friends call me."

"Thank you, Ms. Mayme."

"No, no Miss, just Mayme."

"Okay, Mayme it is. Mayme, you sound a lot like my mom, and I'm going to be honest with you. I got myself into a little trouble, and you seem like the type of person that might give a fellow a second chance."

"I tell you, Sonny, folks in these parts are decent and honest. I am not alone here, as it might look. If you want my help, you'll have to be truthful with me. You do know that the truth sets you free, right?"

Al kind of side stepped and pondered on what this old lady was trying to communicate to him. She wasn't alone, but he sure didn't see a car or any signs of anyone around. Maybe he just needed to get cleaned up and beg for a little food. He did have quite a bit of cash, but this little woman was not to be bought!

"Mayme, what do you say? Would you give me a chance to help out around here?"

"Sonny boy, it sounds like you are the one that needs help!" Something in her heart just melted. He looked like a broken little boy . . . . so sad. "I tell you what, there is an old shower behind the barn, and I'm pretty sure it still works. I'll get you some soap and a towel, and while you get yourself cleaned up, I'll prepare us a bite to eat."

Al was so touched; he could feel the warm tears well up in his eyes. "Mayme, you are an answer to prayer. I could sure use a bite to eat!"

―

It had been over a week now since Kate's death and Eddie's disappearance. John thought he would never get out of this vise of pain that gripped his heart. Officer Nelson had given the "all clear" for things to resume as usual concerning John going back to his home, but it was just an empty house full of nightmares and regrets. Kate's autopsy had revealed some abnormal brain tissue, which raised some questions concerning hemorrhaging. This alone was not significant evidence to suggest the ingestion of drugs, though. And Officer Nelson reiterated once again that no evidence of any kind of drugs were found in the house, so his team of investigators really had nothing to go on at this time. Thank God, the newspapers continued to run an ad with Eddie's picture in the right hand corner of the front page asking for anyone with even a small clue to contact the authorities! John had really beaten himself up concerning Kate's health. She could have very likely had severe medical problems that could have been addressed. Where was he when she needed help so badly, and where was his precious little boy? Over and over John's mind kept him alerted to the fact that this was NOT just a random killing and kidnapping!

So far John simply could not drag himself to the office. He had talked with Anna on several occasions, and she tried to reassure him that his clients were being patient. He knew their sympathy was offered only because there were no real crises in their lives at the moment. The thought had entered his mind to get Anna to contact the law school to solicit the help of one of the students until he could somehow function in the working world again. But for right now, he did not know if there would be any way for him to survive the pain and grief in his life. He simply could not think beyond his brokenness.

—

Belle pulled Eddie close to her as the moonlight spread its glow over the bed where they slept, and watched the dancing shadows in her room from the trees blowing gently beside the window. He had become her world and she his.

Upon arriving at Aunt Van's place, not much had changed except for her Aunt, who had severe dementia. At times Aunt Van did not quite know who Belle was, and at other times, they talked as easily and openly as best friends. Thank God, there were no questions as to who little Eddie was, and why Belle was here. Aunt Van had a young woman living with her named Claire. Claire was so kind and accepting, and she had a small little girl who looked to be four or five. They both treated Aunt Van with affection and much kindness. Everyone called her aunt, "Vannie," so Belle joined in, too, as it seemed to soothe her aunt. Poor Eddie had not said one word, but in the last couple of days, he had warmed up to Dixie, Claire's daughter.

Belle prayed, "Dear Lord, my mind is more confused each day as to how to right my wrongs. I have never been paralyzed in my thought processes as I've been since I took Eddie. I don't even know where to begin to undo all of this. I ask that You have mercy and show me the way, Father."

—

Al and Mayme had become thick as thieves. He had cut the yard, mended the gate and repaired some of the fence out back behind the barn. Mayme had given him some quilts and a pillow to sleep on in the barn, and prepared him three square meals a day. She always reminded him that she was not alone. She also gave him an old ragged Bible. He had never opened his mom's Bible, but he knew his mom to be a God fearing person, and when she died she talked of the angels in her room. She said they had come to take her home. Mayme told him to read the old Bible like a story book. He had read through Genesis, and much of the creation story came back to him from what his mom had related many years ago. Surprisingly, Al found himself most content.

—

"I know it was just a dream, but when I awakened this morning, I felt comforted and at peace about Eddie," Esther whispered to Edmond. "I only wish there were some way I could relate this to John."

"Esther, our son will be comforted by the Holy Spirit. We need only to pray, believe and totally place our trust in God," said Edmond.

"I know, darling, we need only look back on all the times God reigned victoriously when we were in valleys."

Esther let out a long sigh, "Eddie is in our Heavenly Father's Hands and right now we need to focus on how we can encourage our son."

"We have a lot to be thankful for today since John did go to his office . . . that's a start."

"Yes, and he is so fortunate to have Anna working for him. She seems to be a very sincere young woman, and from what I've witnessed, a Christian. Perhaps she'll be someone John could even confide in. He needs a trustworthy friend right now."

Esther poured a second cup of coffee, grabbed her Bible and walked out on the porch to enjoy the gentle breeze while the morning was still cool. This was her favorite time of the day.

—

John was sitting at his desk reflecting on the morning events, and seemed relieved to know he had actually functioned as an attorney for the last several hours. Anna had pored over all the major cases and gotten him up to speed on most everything. They had talked about getting a law student to help in the office part-time, and Anna would check on that. Anna was a gem . . . always so professional and yet gentle and kind. Quite frankly, he did not know if his practice could have survived these past few weeks without her.

John let his mind drift and felt the deep ache in his heart for his son. There was no love any stronger than the love a parent had for their child, but then . . . . what about Kate? Kate was just a child herself. She never had the deep nurturing love of a mother. That was never apparent to him when she was alive. *Oh God, I was so numbed out and out of step with my wife and son. If only, yes if only I had another chance.*

Anna gently tapped on the door and entered John's office. "Mr. Marshall, we have a young man named Daniel Matthews coming in tomorrow at 2:00 to interview for the part-time job."

"Great, Anna, but I have a request, please just call me John. I think you pretty much run this place, you know!"

John let out a small laugh and Anna responded with a gracious smile and nod of her head.

—

Dixie came running to the house with Eddie trailing behind her. She was laughing and galloping like a horse with red clay oozing between her fingers.

"What have you two been up to?" Claire asked in her serious voice, trying to be the authoritative figure, which did not exactly fit her.

"We've been making little baskets and eggs with some red clay we found by the chicken house."

"Dixie, we'll never get that red clay out of your clothes nor Eddie's either."

"Mamma, he likes to eat it! He took the little eggs I had rolled up and ate some of them."

"Well, I don't suppose he'll die from it . . . maybe he is lacking something in his diet. I'll have to mention this to Ms. Belle."

That night at the dinner table, they all had a good laugh about Eddie eating the clay. Dixie said she was going to call him Clay.

Little Eddie laughed to everyone's surprise. Up until now, he had only gone through the motions with no expressions. He had not spoken a single word since Belle had taken him home with her that first night.

Belle's heart was warmed through and through seeing a twinkle in those big brown eyes of Eddie's. He was such a precious little boy. He had the blondest hair, almost white and it had a brightness that looked as though he had a halo hovering above his little noggin.

Belle had been in touch with Sissy, and told her she would be coming into the office next week to play catch up. Belle noticed that Sissy sounded relieved to know that she was coming back. But what she didn't know was that Belle was only coming back to tie up loose ends, pack and move to Calveston.

That night when Belle and Eddie were snuggled up together in bed with Barney stretched out on Belle's feet, Eddie said, "Look at the fingernail moon, Mommy."

Belle was so shocked, she could only remain still while she reveled in the fact that he finally spoke and actually called her "Mommy."

"My sweet boy, yes, I see the fingernail moon. I'm so glad you brought it to my attention. I never thought much about the different stages of the moon, but I promise you I'll always notice in the future. Thank you for telling me."

She held him tight. He said no more, and both dropped off into a peaceful night's sleep.

—

Guy had ceased to see anything in the paper about the Marshall boy, and this was quite a relief to him. It appeared that the police had stashed the case into the "cold files." Maybe he should take another ride over to Albert's place and have a look around.

When he approached the house, he saw that the grass had been recently cut, and the place looked better than he had ever witnessed. He knew

Albert was not a yard person, so what was happening here? Definitely not the time to stop by, as he needed time to digest this surprise!

—

Al and Mayme rarely talked about their personal lives or their past. Since he had been reading the Bible, all conversations revolved around the scriptures and how they related to their personal walk with Jesus. Al's thought processes were so alien to him now, that it was as though he had the brain of someone else. Funny how one event can change your whole life!

Al had called the Walkers who lived across the street from his house in St. Louis, and asked if they would hire someone to keep his place up until he returned. They asked no questions and kindly agreed. He sent them a money order that he obtained from the small post office in Kingston. Actually, he sent them enough money to pay at least three months for yard maintenance, and by then winter would take care of the yard.

Most of the obvious repairs had been completed for Mayme. She kept him fed and gave him more than enough money for supplies, and always insisted that he keep the remainder. She was a saint in every way. A couple of times neighbors had come up unexpectedly, and she remarked that he was her nephew.

No matter how many questions were raised, Mayme always brought the conversation around to the present and spoke about the blessings of the day. Al was sure that she had taught him more about real life than anyone else. Yes, Mayme was a true blessing. He thought for a moment, and marveled at the thoughts that spun around in his head these days. Perhaps he really was a new creature in Christ, as Mayme had shared with him a few days back. Could it be?

—

John had come home early so he could change clothes before going to have dinner at his folks' place. Upon opening the mail, he found the savings account statement, and was shocked to see that it was fifteen thousand dollars less than what he knew the account balance to be. He carefully took note of the two times money had been withdrawn from the account. There was $10,000 withdrawn six weeks prior to another $5,000 withdrawal. The $5,000 was withdrawn a week before Kate's death.

Wow, what in the world would Kate need that much money for! Oh, man, there was so much he did not know about Kate. Actually, the more he thought about it, the more he realized he did not know her at all. How could this be?

John picked up the phone and gave a call to officer Nelson.

"Hi Nelson, this is John Marshall."

"Oh, hi Mr. Marshall. Haven't heard from you in a while. How are you making it, man?"

"Nelson, something very strange has surfaced, and I thought you may have an idea of what this could mean."

"Okay, let's have it."

"Today, when I opened our savings account statement, it was $15,000 less than when I last saw it, and the withdrawals happened before Kate's death. What do you make of that?"

"Maybe we need to talk. Could you come down to the station, John?"

"Sure thing. I'll see you within the hour."

—

Belle was on her way back home. Actually, home now felt more like Aunt Vannie's place. It had been really hard to leave everyone, but she assured them she would return within two weeks. It was a miracle how little Eddie had come around all at once. Actually, everyone called him Clay now. Seemed to fit him, and he responded as though Clay had been his name forever! Thinking back, everything fell into place the night Clay directed her attention to the fingernail moon. When he awoke the next morning, he was throwing the ball to Barney and calling for Dixie. It was like he was alive again. She kept thinking he may start asking questions about his past life, but nothing had come up so far. He seemed like a normal little boy, and so very happy. When she had departed, she told him how much she loved him, and his little face beamed. He said that Dixie was his friend now and he would have fun playing with Dixie and Barney!

This whole new life could only be taken one day at the time. Belle had no long term plan, not one clue as to what their future held.

—

"Officer Nelson, Mr. John Marshall is here to see you," the desk clerk announced.

"Thanks, have him come in please."

"Mr. Marshall, thanks for coming down to the station, I know it was an effort at the end of a work day, but felt we needed to talk in person rather than over the phone."

"What do you make of fifteen thousand dollars being drawn out of this savings account without my having knowledge of such?"

"Well, to be perfectly honest with you, I would have been surprised if this had not surfaced. After talking with your parents, Kate's parents and listening to your account of your wife's behavior, I had a gut feeling that drugs may be the culprit. And with this much money being extracted from your account in such a short time, I would say drugs were at the bottom of everything that happened to your wife and perhaps your son."

"I can't bear to think that Eddie could be in the clutches of a drug dealer or worse. I cannot even go there. To be honest with you, I've wanted to think only that Eddie was being cared for by some very nice person. Especially since his mom and dad were not very nice people."

"John, you are being way too hard on yourself. You were trying to provide for your family. And trusting Kate to be responsible on the domestic front was a normal assessment of things. Sometimes when we do not understand a person's behavior, we question our own selves wondering if it is our problem, and before long the abnormal looks pretty normal to us. That is just human nature."

"Thanks, Officer Nelson, but I still feel very much like a failure, especially regarding my son."

"John, if you don't mind, I would like to personally search your place again. For some reason, I've felt all along that there is evidence lurking somewhere on your place. Would it be okay if I came by sometime this week while you are working?"

"Sure, here is an extra key to our house. Take your time. I wish you luck . . . . we sure need some, don't we?"

Daniel Matthews was working out great so far in the law office. Anna could depend on him to run all courthouse errands and handle filings. She now had plenty of time to take care of all the legal documents and submit them to Mr. Marshall. She still found herself calling him Mr. Marshall although he reminded her to just call him John. She had been thinking lately about inviting him to visit her church. At times she could detect a deep sadness in him, and she knew that only the peace of Jesus could help that hollowness in his heart. She prayed for him often. Actually, to be perfectly honest, she thought of him a little too often. He was six years older than she and given the recent tragedy in his life, she realized any romantic thoughts were probably not God's Will at this time, but she could not deny that she was drawn to him.

—

Guy could not hold off any longer, he would have to do a little investigating himself regarding Albert's whereabouts. As he drove past Albert's house, he had an idea.

Turning around, he drove up the driveway of a neighbor's house.

"Yes, hello, uh sir, I'm looking for my good friend Albert Statham. Would you happen to know if he has moved?"

"Young man, I haven't seen Albert in quite a while. By the way my name is Henry. I don't believe I got yours."

"My name is Jimmy."

"Well, Jimmy, you might check across the street with the Walkers because they have been keeping up Albert's yard."

"Great, okay, thank you, sir. Bye."

Guy went across the way and knocked on the Walkers' door. He just knew this was the break he needed. No answer.

"Fine, I'll come back tomorrow." Guy muttered under his breath.

—

Officer Nelson decided to check with some of his undercover guys. Maybe they could come up with something that would help open a door in the Marshalls' case. Prior to his talk with John Marshall, things had been at a total stand still. Learning that drugs could have played a big part changed the fabric of everything. Talk could be bought and his guys had paid handsomely before for good solid evidence, which ultimately solved or at least helped their cases. He was still puzzled as to why someone dealing in drugs would have kidnapped a young child, though. That sort of thing usually cannot be kept quiet within the grapevine, plus drug dealing and selling kids were two separate categories.

He knew he needed to go through the Marshalls' house one more time, but this week had been pulling at him from all angles. He promised himself to not let this week get by without doing a final search!

Belle's first day back in the office was the most frenetic she could ever remember. Her office looked as though she had been gone six months with stacks of papers to sign and files to review, plus meetings with Starnes and Sissy. She noticed a stack of outdated newspapers piled on the corner of her desk, and knew she needed to face facts. She searched through until she located the papers from the first two weeks of June. Oh, my goodness, there was his precious little face with notice of a reward for any clues regarding his whereabouts. Then her eyes focused on the name John Marshall, an attorney here in the city, who was the father of this little boy. She wanted to die in her agony. Clay has a dad, and that dad has died a million deaths over his missing son. *Lord, forgive me, please forgive me for causing so much pain for others. Please help me get through this, Father. I beg you. And Lord, one more thing, give comfort and peace to the heart of Clay's dad.*

She had to somehow pull herself together and focus on the things at hand in the office. The most immediate situation to be addressed was the adoption of a young boy through the Welfare Department. Starnes had interviewed Mr. & Mrs. Hamilton twice and made a decision in favor of them unless Belle had any objections. Belle well remembered interviewing the couple. Mrs. Hamilton had seemed desperate for a child, and at the time that had not set well with her, but thinking about the whole situation now, she felt totally different. She had told Starnes, he made a good decision, and she really meant it. Sissy had finalized all the paper work to insure that the adoption would be smooth, as usual. She would give the Hamiltons a call in a few days to pick up the completed paper work, and the couple would have their little boy.

Belle thought, "If it were only that easy for me."

Guy was back again in Albert's neighborhood. He pulled up to the Walkers and saw an old man out back sitting in a rocking chair.

"Hey there! Are you Mr. Walker?"

"Who would be asking, son?"

"The name is Jimmy, and I'm looking for my good friend Albert."

"Haven't seen Albert around lately."

"Do you know where he is or when he could be coming back? Mr. Henry said you were keeping up the yard for him while he is away."

"Yep, that's right. Told me he was doing some traveling, so I don't rightly know when he'll be back."

"I sure would like to give him the money I owe him. You don't happen to know where I might find him, do you?"

"Nope. The only thing I know is that when he sent me money to get the grass cut, the envelope was postmarked Kingston, Texas, but that's been a few weeks ago."

Guy could hardly contain himself. He knew exactly where to find the little sleepy community of Kingston. If Albert was still there, he would be dead meat!

"Mayme, you are the best cook in the world, did you know that?"

"There you go again . . . . what do you want now, Sonny boy?"

"What I want is for you to tell me the truth."

"The truth about what?"

"About Jesus. I'll never be worthy enough for Him to love me, Mayme."

"You just hold on a minute, Sonny boy. I'll be right back."

Mayme had been praying and waiting for this moment. She knew the Holy Spirit was in the driver's seat, so she opened her old family Bible to John 3:3. "A personal relationship with God begins with an event Jesus referred to as a new birth. Only when we are born spiritually into God's family do we become His children and members of His spiritual Kingdom."

"Young man, you must admit your need. We come into this world physically alive, but spiritually dead. The Bible says, 'All have sinned and fall short of the glory of God.' Romans 3:23. 'There is none righteous, no, not one' Romans 3:10 and 'The wages of sin is death.'"

"Mayme, I feel like my sins have already sentenced me to death here and eternity, too."

"Listen to God's Word, Al. God loved us enough to send His own Son into this world to rescue us from the devastating effects of our sin. Jesus died in our place, offering Himself as the perfect sacrifice to pay the price of sin. He paid for the least and the worst of our sins."

"Even a criminal like me, Mayme?"

"No one is saved by being good. We are saved by trusting in Christ. The Bible says, 'For by grace you have been saved through faith, and that not of yourselves; it is the gift of God, not of works, lest anyone should boast' Ephesians 2:8-9."

"I have done some horrible things in my past, Mayme. Do you really think God can forgive me?"

"Al, the Bible says in John 3:16, 'For God loved the world so much that he gave his only Son so that anyone who believes in him shall not perish but have eternal life.' Would you like to ask God to forgive you, and accept Jesus as your savior, Al?"

"More than anything, yes ma'am, I would."

"I wrote this sinner's prayer down many years ago in the front of my Bible, and if you would like to read this prayer to the Lord, I'm sure He'll meet you halfway, Al."

Al took the old family Bible, hugged it tight, and dropped to his knees with tears streaming down his face.

"God, I know I have sinned against You. I do believe that Jesus is your Son, that He died for my sins, and that He rose from the dead to prove it. Now, God, I accept your Son, Jesus, as Your gift for my salvation."

Mayme reached down and placed her hand on his head and prayed blessings on this new creature in Christ, and asked God to make all the crooked places straight in Al's life, and that from this day forward he would pursue Jesus at any cost.

Something funny struck Al and he said, "You know, Mayme, now I understand when you said you were not alone here. It is because you have Jesus with you, isn't it?"

"That is God's truth, Sonny boy."

"Mayme, how will I ever thank you enough for getting me on the right road?"

"Son, it is all about thanking and praising our Heavenly Father. Really pretty simple!"

Later on that night, Al decided to place his pallet outside and sleep under the stars.

There was really nothing that could hurt him, and if it did, he knew to be absent from the body meant to be present with the Lord. Funny how God brought things from the scripture so clearly to mind.

Lord, was it Your plan all along for me to meet Mayme, so she could help me find You or did You find me at Your appointed time? You know, I'm really in a lot of trouble, and it is mostly with Guy. I know in my heart I did not kill anyone. That knife was flying every direction and Mrs. Marshall was just acting wild. I really think she had mixed drugs and gotten herself into some trouble. You know, I only turned her hand, and the way she jumped at me, the knife punctured the side of her stomach. I don't know how she could have died from that wound, though, but she did. I knew she was dead before I left. Lord, if she had been alive, I hope I would have helped her. Do You think I would have Lord? These are the kind of thoughts that haunt me, God. Please give me Your Peace, sweet Jesus.

Belle had been home for a little over two weeks, and practically every minute of her time had been spent at the office. All important documentation had been handled. She had told Sissy and Starnes that her only living relative needed a care giver, and she felt compelled to take care of her. The whole office was in a state of shock since her two week notice gave little or no time for someone to make a seamless transition into her position. Her guess would be that Sissy could handle quite a few things, and Starnes could take care of the rest until they could hire the right person. She did not allow herself to feel the least bit of guilt.

When she talked to her landlord regarding breaking her lease, he was most understanding and waived all penalties. She decided to give him her furniture. There really wasn't any time to sell it, and she could not manage the details of moving it. The furniture was contemporary and would probably help furnish a couple of apartments. She had packed up a few boxes of special dishes and sentimental things and placed them in the trunk. The back seat was loaded down with her wardrobe and books.

It was almost 7:00 p.m. and the cleaning people would be coming soon. Belle was going through the last stack of documents to sign off on. She took everything to Sissy's desk and arranged neat piles, plus a personal note of thanks to Sissy. As she positioned the "thank you" note by Sissy's phone, she noticed the "Hamilton" file. Upon opening the file, there lay a certified copy of the birth record for the child the Hamiltons had adopted. She looked closer, and suddenly it dawned on her that she may need a birth certificate for Clay! Certainly, this little boy was close to the same age, and since Hamilton was the last name, it just might work! The birth certificate had John Clayton Hamilton as the little boy's name. "I can't believe this fell into my hands, dear Lord," Belle let out a little squeal of glee. "Sissy will spend most of the morning looking for this tomorrow, but I'm confident she will surmise she must have mistakenly tossed it into the paper shredder bin with other papers! I can't believe it!" Suddenly Belle's heavy heart lifted, and she could hardly wait to get on the road to see her family.

John had a copy of Kate's obituary on the corner of his desk. He could not bring himself to place it somewhere else. Kate was the link to his son, he felt sure and now she was gone. At times when he reflected on the events after Kate's death, it was all like a dream, just so unreal.

It had been a short service with just his friends and immediate family at her funeral. It broke his heart to realize that Kate had no friends, and he had been too busy to emotionally support her. His grief for Eddie was unending. Work kept him sane. He rarely went home. Most of his clothes were at his parents' house. His mom had insisted, and he had to admit whenever he arrived at their place, no matter the hour, there was always a plate of food left on the stove for him. His parents did not intrude. Their way was quiet, but encouraging and nurturing to his contrite spirit. They rarely discussed Eddie, just as they rarely discussed Kate's death. To John both seemed to be dead. His hopes of finding Eddie had been dashed when Officer Nelson discovered cocaine and narcotics in the bottom of Kate's chest in their closet. It was her personal chest of memorabilia, along with scarves and caps. After Officer Nelson had knowledge of the substantial amounts withdrawn from their savings, he did not stop his search until evidence surfaced.

A light tap on the door brought John back to the moment. "Hi, Mr. Marshall, hope I'm not disturbing you," Daniel said softly.

"Yes, Daniel, please come in."

"I wanted to invite you to a Bible study I'm starting in my home on Thursday evenings."

"Daniel, I just don't know how to be sociable anymore. My mind seems to be functional at the office, but when I'm not absorbed in my work, I seem to be in some kind of stupor."

"It will only be a handful of people. Most of them are students at the law school where I attend. Perhaps you could give them some guidance."

"You know, Daniel, you have an intentional relationship with Jesus. It is so easy to see. I don't even have a relationship with Him. I'm certain I would not be able to contribute anything to anyone right now."

"Well, at least think about it. It may be something that could fill a void in your life right now. And by the way, Dr. Garrison has called several times. He has been very concerned about you. He must be a caring soul since he hasn't even met you and still continues to call."

"Thanks, Daniel, I'll give him a call this afternoon. And by the way, you and Anna simply cannot be replaced. I feel like you have carried my practice for me. We really need to sit down and have a talk about your staying on after you take the bar exam."

"Thanks, Mr. Marshall, I would love to continue to work with you."

Daniel exited John's office with such ease and grace. He was just the kind of man John always aspired to be, and yet so miserably failed. Maybe it was time to call Dr. Garrison and set up an appointment for himself.

—

Guy was entering the little sleepy town of Kingston with different scenarios of Albert's demise being replayed in his head. A good place to start would be the local grocery store and then perhaps a service station. He just needed to appear a good hearted soul looking for his best friend. As he stepped up to the only cashier in the small grocery store, a young girl gave him a sweet smile and asked if he needed some assistance.

Guy shot back a wide grin and said, "I hope you can help me find a good buddy of mine. His name is Albert, and I believe he may have moved here a few weeks back."

The young girl said, "I would not know anyone new by that name. I'm sorry."

"Well, Albert is in his late twenties with auburn hair."

"Maybe I saw him a couple of times, but not lately."

"Can you think of someone else who may be able to help me?"

"Sorry, I cannot."

Guy decided to stop at a hardware store a couple of doors down. As he entered the door, a friendly face appeared immediately and asked could he help.

"As a matter of fact, you can. I've been trying to locate a good friend, and I was told he may be here in Kingston. His name is Albert Statham, mid twenties with sandy colored hair."

"Yea, I know who you are talking about, but I haven't seen him recently. He was helping out Ms. Mayme with some odd jobs, but like I said, I don't recollect seeing him lately."

"Maybe you could tell me where Ms. Mayme lives."

"Well, as the crow flies, it is about two miles from here. Just go to the end of Main, take a right onto the highway, then go about two miles, take a left on a gravel road, and Ms. Mayme's would be about 2 miles on the right before you get to the dead end."

"Man, I sure do thank you. I'll be on my way."

"Your friend really seemed like a nice guy!"

Guy muttered under his breath, "nice guy and dead guy."

The directions from the man at the hardware store were right on target. Guy decided to drive to the end of the road and turn around before stopping at the weathered looking house. He drove back slowly looking for evidence of Albert or his vehicle. He parked his car on the gravel road and walked up to the front porch. Before he got to the door, it swung wide open and an elderly woman stepped out.

"I don't believe we've had the privilege of meeting before, young man. May I help you?"

"I'm looking for a good friend of mine named Albert, Albert Statham. The gentleman at the hardware store said you might know where he would be since he did some work for you."

"Yes, I remember Albert well. He was a most disturbed young man."

"Yea, that would be Albert . . . . just a little crazy, if you know what I mean."

"I'm sorry, I don't think I got your name."

"You can just call me Guy."

"Well, Guy, Albert did stay for a while, and he helped me with some repairs, but one day a couple of weeks ago, he had a change of heart and I've not seen that young man since."

"Did he say where he was going?"

"No, didn't say a word about where he was going, but I really don't expect to ever see him again. I never even knew where he came from, but I doubt he journeys back wherever it was."

"Well, I'll be going my way."

"God bless you, young man."

Guy felt his heart grow ice cold. God was the last subject he wanted to hear or talk about . . . . rubbish.

—

Belle was growing more excited by the moment! She was headed down the long driveway to Aunt Vannie's. As she was coming to a stop she saw Clay and Dixie running towards her car. Dixie squealed, "Welcome home Ms. Belle!"

Clay stepped very slowly from Dixie's grasp and moved close to the car door. When Belle opened the door, he lifted his little arms as she bent down to pull him close to her. They embraced for what seemed to be a lifetime. Belle knew now that there was no turning back. She would do everything in her power to promote a promising future for this precious little boy, even if it meant sacrificing her life!

Claire came to the door, and welcomed Belle with the good news that dinner was almost prepared.

Belle took the kids in to get them washed up and freshen up a bit herself. She felt like a giddy school girl. This house was so full of love!

As they sat at the dining room table, Aunt Vannie decided to say the blessing.

"Dear Lord, we thank you for bringing our precious Belle back safely. May she never leave us again. Thank you for the hands that prepared this food, and lead us in the paths of righteousness for Your Name's sake. Amen."

Belle was stunned. Aunt Vannie seemed so perfectly lucid, which she had not witnessed before her departure a couple of weeks back. This was truly a miracle!

"Aunt Vannie, you seem to be feeling very well. I believe these galloping kids have kept you entertained and Claire has to be the best care giver ever! I'm so pleased."

"You know, Belle, youth is life! Just being around your family and young people does the heart good."

"In your case, it has done wonders for your health! Perhaps you and I can talk later after the children have been tucked in . . . . I would love that."

"That would be nice, Belle."

—

Mayme walked out to the barn after the stranger disappeared down the road headed back to town.

"Al, are you aware a man named Guy is looking for you?"

"I figured he would find me one day, Mayme, and I know he is up to no good. He is a drug dealer who I used to run drugs for, but those days are gone, thanks to you and the Lord."

"Well, I told this fellow you had a change of heart, and it had been a couple of weeks since I had seen the man he was looking for. And, we both know that's the truth because you are a new creature in Christ. All things are new; the old has passed away."

"Mayme, you saved my skin. But you know the odd thing is I'm no longer anxious or afraid because my life is God's, and whatever he does regarding my life is okay by me. I'm sure there will always be consequences for my sins, but I have no guilt or shame for I know I'm forgiven. I suppose to live a life, one will always have some regrets, but with God's help we can lift up our heads and praise Him with joyful hearts. Mayme, what a great God we have!"

"Al, how would you like to start going to church with me?"

"Do you really mean it?"

"Why sure, I do!"

"Well, Mayme, this Sunday you've got a date!"

—

John was leaving his office when Anna asked him if he would like to attend church with her on Sunday.

"Anna, I have not thought about going to church in so long, I really don't know how I feel about going this Sunday. Perhaps I need more time."

"I'll check with you again, okay?"

"Alright. By the way, I'm going to see Dr. Garrison, so I probably will not be back until tomorrow. You have a nice evening, Anna."

"You, too, John."

He felt good when she called him John. Actually, he felt comforted just being around Anna when he was at the office. She was always concerned and extended herself in going beyond the call of duty. Lately, he had wondered if he actually had feelings for this young woman, and that was something he probably needed to talk over with Dr. Garrison. He just needed to talk with someone who would listen to his head full of guilt and heart full of grief and shame.

—

Belle was sitting in one of the rockers on Aunt Vannie's front porch reflecting on the past few weeks. Life just seemed to be hurtling by her, and whenever it looked as though a breath might be in sight, another hurdle popped up to challenge her heart and wits.

The day she had returned, Aunt Vannie had been so alert and talkative. Belle was looking forward to having a nice conversation with her aunt after getting Clay to bed, but when she entered the living room, her aunt was slumped over in her little glider. Belle had rushed to her side and tried to lift her head, but it was too late. It had all been such a shock!

There had been so many details to tend to that she could hardly stop to think how little Clay's and Dixie's emotions were handling all of this. The two busied themselves outside mostly. They were constantly together. Whenever you saw one the other was close behind. Claire had been her stronghold. She knew where Aunt Vannie's important papers were. She knew the preacher and several of Aunt Vannie's close friends who were still living. Claire had gently guided Belle through all the details, visitation and the funeral. Many of the people in the community brought food, and some even continued to stop by and check to see if they could help in any way. Belle honestly felt loved. It had been so many years since she felt the warmth of affectionate people in her life.

Aunt Vannie had bequeathed the place to Belle as well as leaving her money from investments and savings. Her will also made mention of monetary provisions for Claire, for which Belle was thankful. Claire had totally devoted the last few years to her aunt, and made this place a home full of love and acceptance. How did Aunt Vannie scrimp and save as she had . . . . .I wonder. Apparently, her aunt had been a very smart individual or perhaps she was just one of those wise souls, who did not need much to live on. She seemed to thrive on the simple things of life.

"What next, dear Lord? Where do we go from here or do we just stay and rest here for a season?"

1988

Esther and Edmond sat in the sun room sharing conversation and tea. The morning was sunny and full of hope for a grand day. This was their favorite time together.

"Thanks, Esther for making our home so warm and comfortable. A man could not wish for more."

"I so wish our son had a real home," Esther whispered.

"I can see some subtle differences in John lately. Haven't you noticed?" asked Edmond.

"Maybe a little."

"I have heard him make a few casual statements regarding Anna, too!"

Esther paused for a moment. "I don't know if our son can move on to a new life without having closure on his son's disappearance or kidnapping, but I dare not bring any of this up because I fear John is so fragile he will fall apart regarding any discussion concerning Eddie."

"That is something only the Lord can take care of. I have a hard time dealing with all of this myself. I guess the thing that causes me the most grief is the fact that Kate was so sick and ill equipped to take care of Eddie, but we did not realize it. John must have struggled mightily under that facade of pride."

"Edmond, let's continue to pray that our Heavenly Father will bring about healing to all of us. I will say this, John seems to be less restless since he has been going to Daniel's Bible study on Thursday nights. We all need to fill our lives each day with worthy activities that will allow the love of God to flow through us to others."

"You are a wise woman, Esther. I'm sure that's the reason I married you in the first place!"

"Yea, right!"

"I think I heard the phone. I'll be right back."

Esther returned with a broad smile on her face. "Miracles never cease. You'll never believe it! That was John, and he asked if I would mind if he brought Anna home for dinner tonight. Oh, Edmond, God is so good."

John sat at his desk smiling mildly and hoping that he had not jumped to any conclusions regarding Anna's feelings toward him. It was hard to believe that only six months ago, he had casually attended church with her, then committed to being a part of the Bible study at Dan's place, and now inviting her to dinner with his parents so they could get to know her.

It was also hard to believe a year had passed since Kate's death and Eddie's disappearance. The only way he could handle things was to take one day at a time. Anna had been his stronghold since the very beginning. She was young, but strong in the Lord with a beautiful spirit. He really relied on her emotional support, although he never talked about the past, she seemed to know where his heart was during the silent times, and her presence gave him great comfort. He wondered how a woman of such substance would want such a broken man as he was, and perhaps always would be.

Several weeks ago Dan had a slip-up and confirmed what John thought he knew. Yes, Anna was in love with him. Dan said it only took him a few weeks to recognize how much Anna embraced John in everything she did.

Well, tonight would be a welcomed change for his parents. Perhaps that infectious laugh of Anna's would have a healing effect on all of them!

Anna quietly opened his office door. "John, just a reminder that you have an appointment with Dr. Garrison at 3:00."

"Thanks for the reminder, and don't forget, I'll pick you up around 6:00 and we'll join Mom and Dad for dinner."

"How could I forget! I've been looking forward to one of your mother's wonderful meals you are always raving about. What a treat! See you at six."

John thought, "She is so full of joy. That's it . . . joy of the Lord!"

—

Belle could see Clay getting excited in the back seat as they were approaching Claire and Dixie's little place. They always rode together to church every Sunday, and if Dixie and Clay had not seen each other during the week, they were a real handful during church! Dixie was five, and would start to school soon. Belle knew that Clay would be lost for a while without his little buddy. They were good for each other and good to each other. Belle had never heard them say an unkind word or have any kind of squabble. Dixie had jet black hair and huge deep blue eyes. Clay had platinum hair with large deep brown eyes. What a pair!

"Okay, Clay, be a gentleman and go knock on the door," Belle said as they neared Claire's place.

She opened the car door for him, and he went running to the front door calling for Dixie. She opened the door with a squeal. "Hi! Are we going to play after church?"

Clay looked back toward the car as if asking Belle what he should say, then said, "Mom won't say no."

Belle waved for everyone to get in the car. "If we don't hurry, we'll end up sitting in the front pew, and you guys know what that means . . . . .total quietness! Hi Claire. Hey sweet Dixie! Okay, here we go!"

Touching Belle on the shoulder, Claire said, "It is so good to see you two. Sorry we haven't been to visit, but I've stayed close to home because of some repairs that were being done. During our last storm one of the large trees split, fell on the roof and caused a substantial leak."

"Is everything okay now?" Belle asked.

"It is and you know who came to check on us?"

"Hmmm. I guess that would be our handsome pastor, right?"

"How did you know?"

"Just a guess when I saw that twinkle in your eye!"

"Stop it, Belle!"

"Well, he is single and you are available."

"Belle, I don't think I'm the type to be a pastor's wife."

"And why not?"

Claire looked back to make sure the children were not tuned in to her conversation. "You know my past is stained."

"Claire, what living soul does not have regrets over their mistakes. Surely, you've been listening to the sermons. We are new creatures in Christ."

"You know, Belle, you've really matured in your spiritual walk these last few months. I can remember not too long ago when you hardly expressed yourself, and just listen to all this good advice now! It is hard to remember when you and Clay were not in our lives. Please never entertain the thought of leaving, okay?"

"No promises about the future, but for now we're living the moment and grateful for all of God's blessings."

Later that night when Belle was reflecting on their Sabbath, she noticed a "fingernail" moon as Clay would call it. He still slept with her. Barney had decided two was company and three a crowd, so he had started sleeping on the rug beside their bed. She was always haunted by the thought of Clay remembering the life he had before she came into his life, but she never saw any signs of him being unhappy or perplexed over anything. Actually, he was the most well adjusted individual she had ever known. He never met a stranger, and everyone enjoyed being around him.

—

Officer Nelson debated on how to share this latest news with John Marshall. There simply was no way to soften things or skirt the issue concerning little Eddie's case being at a dead end as far as the police force was concerned.

Picking up the phone, he dialed John's office and took a deep breath.

"Hey John, this is Nelson over at the police precinct."

"Hi Officer Nelson, you know, I was just thinking about calling you!"

"Well, let me catch you up on what my narc guys have come up with. For several months we've had a hunch about the drug dealer who Mrs. Marshall probably secured her drugs from. We haven't been able to gather enough evidence to bring this fellow in for questioning, but we have watched him day and night. Anyway, around noon yesterday, there did not seem to be much stirring at his house, so a couple of our guys decided to pay him a visit. When he did not answer the door, they went in through a back window, and found a white male around thirty-five years old dead on the kitchen floor, which we discovered later was from an overdose."

"Do you think this man could have kidnapped my little boy?"

"John, we don't know, but we do know the grade of cocaine we found in his house was the same poor grade that we discovered in your home. I can tell you this, we combed the entire house and garage, and there was no sign of a small child having been there."

"What am I supposed to surmise from this information, Nelson?"

"John, I'm sorry. I know you do not view this as good news, but just maybe your little boy was not kidnapped by a low lying drug dealer. You know we had several neighbors who worried about your son roaming the neighborhood, and your wife's death and your son's disappearance could be totally unconnected."

"I don't think I'll have closure on any of this until I find my son, Nelson!"

"John, I'm sorry. I am so sorry, but unless something surfaces from street talk, we may be at a dead end."

"I know the feeling," John sighed.

—

Al's life had changed so much since he met Mayme that he could hardly remember his past. They never talked about it, and oddly enough, the people in the community accepted him as Mayme's nephew, which of course, he was not, but neither one of them had any family so it felt good to claim that they were kin!

He had joined the little country church, and volunteered to do the yard work and also paint the exterior of the church. The local Revel Hardware store had hired him to work in the stock room. He never seemed to tire and always volunteered to do extra things for Mr. Gibbs, the owner. When he was given a raise, he decided to pay Mayme for room and board. She really fought him about this, but he insisted.

Al had talked it over with Mayme and she agreed that a truck would be useful to haul things for the church and the store, too. After much thought and prayer, he decided to sell his car and buy a small used truck. It had been difficult to sell his mom's car, but he had moved on and needed to close that chapter of his life. He got a good price for it – enough to pay cash for his truck, and have a little left. He had treated Mayme to a meal at the little diner in town, and then taken her to Cindy's Closet, a ladies' apparel shop a couple of doors down from his work. He had talked with Cindy before hand and given her $200.00 so Mayme could get a few things.

As time marched on Mayme and Al were more like family and everyone in the community and their church treated them as mother and son. Al mentioned to Mayme one afternoon while they were sitting on the porch that he probably needed to take a couple of days off and go home. Her face suddenly looked like stone, and he had immediately told her it was just to tie up some loose ends regarding the sale of his house, then he would be returning. Funny, he had never seen Mayme as being frail, but he could see now that he needed to be protective of her. He truly wished he had been able to take care of his own mother as he had Mayme.

"Okay, Mayme, I'm off to the big city and will be right back here on this front porch within five days, okay?"

"Don't go speeding, you hear me, Sonny boy?"

"You just say those prayers, and I'll be fine!"

—

Belle had basically been a kid with Clay for the last two weeks, since Dixie had started to school. It was plain to see he missed his little buddy. Life had settled into a regular routine, and for some reason Belle was beginning to feel a little restless. She loved her time with Clay and all of his delightful discoveries on their little farm, but still she desired a bit of a challenge. She had thought about getting riding lessons for Clay and herself. Who knows, if they enjoyed riding maybe she would purchase a couple of horses.

That night at the table, Belle broached the subject, "Clay, I've been thinking about buying a couple of horses . . . . one for you and one for me. What do you think?"

"Oh, Mom, that would be fun, and then Dixie could ride my horse."

"Well, of course, dear, but you know what we are going to do first?"

Clay just stared at Belle with those penetrating brown eyes and shook his head, no.

"You and I are going to learn how to ride a horse. I've been thinking about asking Mr. Samuels if he could teach us how to ride one of his gentle horses, maybe even start you out on a pony. How would that be?"

Clay gave a wide grin and clapped his hands with gusto!

"Okay, it is a deal. Tomorrow we'll take a ride to Mr. Samuels, and ask if he has time to give us riding lessons!"

Leslie Samuels had a small ranch three miles down the road from Belle's. He had worked hard and perhaps smart the last ten years or so, and was known for his excellent breed of quarter horses. Ranchers and cattlemen kept him in business, and on the side he had won more than his fair share of prize money from barrel racing.

Leslie had met Belle when her aunt passed away, and slowly gotten acquainted with her while attending church services and other community functions. Belle was difficult to read and hard to get close to. She was friendly enough, but still there was always this barricade that he had never gotten through. For some reason, he felt she was very fragile behind that fortress of a facade. If he were honest with himself, he was extremely attracted to Belle. Actually, he had been trying to get the courage to ask her out for dinner. And perhaps the reason he had not was because she and Clay were always involved with Clay's interests. He had never seen anyone so devoted to a child! Oh, well, God would open a door in His timing.

Belle and Clay both jumped out of the car once they parked in Leslie Samuels' driveway. Clay had been one ball of excitement since Belle discussed riding lessons and buying a couple of horses.

Leslie Samuels opened his front door wide and Clay ran right in. When Belle got to the door, she suddenly seemed at a loss for words, and that was so unlike her!

Belle extended her hand and greeted Leslie. "Well, I hope we are not barging in; I really need to get a telephone line installed so I can give folks fair warning of my arrival!"

Leslie grinned and shook her hand with one hand and covered hers with his other hand. "Come in and I'll pour up something cool to drink. Hey Clay, what flavor Kool Aid do you want, my man?"

"Have you got grape?" Clay asked rather shyly, now that Mr. Samuels was personally addressing him.

"I just happen to have grape and orange. How about you, Belle?"

Belle announced, "Grape will be just fine, Leslie."

"I tell you what, let's take our drinks out on the screened-in porch. Clay, you'll be able to see some of the new colts in the pasture from there!"

"He and I both would love that, and since horses are your business, we really need your advice."

"I'll sure help if I can." Leslie was just thanking the Lord for a subject that he knew a little about.

"Here's the deal," Belle said. "Since Dixie is in school this year and Clay does not start until the following, he seems a little lost. Plus I've come to the realization that I need to get my teeth into something as well. So, we were thinking about asking you to give us riding lessons for starters. Then perhaps we could purchase a couple of horses."

"Wow, Belle, that sounds terrific. I'm excited that you are interested in quarter horses!"

"I guess you could say at this point, just any horse. I really have limited knowledge regarding the different breeds of horses."

"Well, I believe we have just the horse for Clay to start out on today. Are you ready, buddy?"

Clay firmly placed his glass of Kool Aid on the little porch table and ran for the back door!

"Leslie, I didn't mean to interrupt your schedule today. We can do this at your convenience and set up something weekly."

"Belle, this is perfect timing. I don't have one thing on my calendar for today. And by the way, please just call me Les. That is what I've been called most of my life."

"Okay, Les. I'm excited about Clay being able to ride a horse today, but you know this child is my life, so you must be sure he has a very gentle ride!"

John was reflecting on the wonderful time he and Anna had enjoyed with his parents a few weeks back. There was such an ease about everything. His parents connected so genuinely with Anna and the conversation was light and yet rich. All four of them had a grand time. He had not seen his mom smile as she did in perhaps years. Certainly, they must have sensed he and Kate were never happy. Every time he had a passing thought of Kate, his heart ached for Eddie until he thought it might burst! How would he make it without his son?

Anna popped her head in his office and reminded him of his appointment with Dr. Garrison.

"Oh, yes, thanks, Anna. See you at Dan's for our Bible class tonight?"

"Wouldn't miss it for the world!"

John drove slowly to Dr. Garrison's office in deep thought and saddled with guilt. He was the last patient for the afternoon. The receptionist greeted him, and said Dr. Garrison would only be a few more moments. She politely said good-bye and left for the day.

"Hey John, how are you?"

"Okay, I guess. How is your day going Dr. Garrison?"

"Not too bad. What do you say we just have our chat here in the reception area. It is so comfortable and the view is much better. We have the place to ourselves."

"Fine with me."

"What's on your mind, John? You seem a little preoccupied."

"That heavy load of guilt over Kate and the terrible pain and anguish over Eddie's disappearance. And then on the other side of the coin, there is Anna, who you know I simply adore. And the strange thing is when I'm with her, it's as though I'm someone else. I can almost escape from the grief and hurt of losing Eddie. At times I think I'm ready to ask Anna to marry me, and then at other times I think about how unfair that may be to her, if I should get bogged down in my losses and overcome with grief. I've tossed it back and forth quite a bit these past couple of weeks."

"John, how would you feel or handle life if Anna were not in your life?"

"Oh, yes, that would be a very sad day, Dr. Garrison. But I know from a Christian's standpoint, I need to seek wholeness in my relationship with the Lord, not Anna."

"John, do you know what a difference there is in your life from the first time I met you compared to the present? Quite a bit of emotional healing has come about, and I've witnessed a spiritual maturity in you that few people possess."

"One day at a time . . . . that's all I can do, and that is why it is difficult for me to be optimistic about providing a great future for Anna."

"John, let me say this, not as your doctor, but as your friend. You nor I can provide a future for anyone. God is the one who provides for all of us, and perhaps it is time you trusted God for His provisions for Anna's future, too."

"That is wise advice, Dr. Garrison, and I appreciate your being so candid with me. This will be a matter of prayer, and too, I want to discuss my thoughts with my folks. I've kept them at arm's length for so many years, and I now realize I could have used much of their wise experience along the way, but was just too proud to ask. False pride has been one of the worst sins of my life. I just thank God for giving me another chance. You know, it seems like I remember asking God for a second chance not so long ago."

"John, give this to God, and trust Him for clarity. Just give me a call should you feel the need to talk. I really do not think you need to schedule routine visits, anymore."

"Are you sure?"

"Yes, very. So long, John and God bless."

"Thanks for everything, Dr. Garrison."

John decided to stop by the office on his way home. When he was fumbling with his office keys, Dan all but ran over him exiting the door.

"Man, what's the hurry?" As soon as he saw Dan's expression, he knew something was wrong. "Dan, what is it?"

"Hurry, just come with me, and we'll talk on the way! I'll drive."

John climbed into Dan's car and prayed that whatever was wrong, God would make right!

"Okay, John, I hate to tell you this, but I just received a call from Memorial Hospital. Anna has been in a pretty bad wreck."

"Is she alive?"

"Yes, but seriously injured. The head physician of the emergency room called our office asking for you. When I told him you were not there, he related what he knew at the time."

"Did he say she would be okay?"

"He had to go, so that's all I know, John."

"Dan, I do not know what I would do if something happened to Anna. I simply cannot take any more!"

As sure as his word, Al drove back to Kingston five days after his departure, and that sweet Mayme was in her rocking chair on the porch waiting for his return. They embraced and she went inside to fetch him a cup of tea. They had a "spot of tea" ritual most afternoons when he came in from work. She had spoiled him for so long, and now he just wanted to spoil her. If it had not been for her where would his soul be?

They talked so easily, and most of the time it was about the simple blessings of the day, pretty weather, a gentle breeze, fall colors or the fresh smell of recently cut grass. There was always something to thank the good Lord for in their conversations.

"I'm so glad to be home, Mayme."

"Are you going to be making any more trips so far away again?"

"Don't think so. Everything is closed regarding the house, and I hauled the majority of our belongings in the house to the Salvation Army. I brought a few things back with me. Mom's old chest and her Bible are in the truck along with a few clothes of mine. I have closed that chapter of my life, Mayme, and all I want is what God desires for me."

"Well, Sonny boy, I know someone who is very interested in getting to know you!"

"And who would that be?"

"Cindy. When she was helping me select a couple of dresses at her shop, she had a real curiosity about you. Wanted to know if you had been married, did you have children, etc. You get the picture?"

"What did you tell her?"

"I just told her that you were a child of God intent on doing His will, and I thought you may be an available gentleman."

"Don't know if I can live up to all that!"

"If you would like to ask her over for dinner one evening, I'll prepare something fancy!"

"Everything you fix is fancy, Mayme! And before I forget it, I want us to open up an account at the bank together. I want you to be able to get money whenever you need it from my account. I'll be depositing thirty thousand dollars in our account. I plan to really fix up this place. We'll put our heads together and prioritize and I'll focus on working here at the house on the week-ends."

"Al, truly, you are a new creature. Christ has so totally transformed you, son. But you know that I cannot spend your money. I have enough. God always supplies my needs, just don't want for a thing."

"Mayme, we must think of the future, too. If anything were to happen to me, I would want you to be able to have access to my funds. No further discussion, now. I'll break for lunch in the morning around 11:00, and we'll be going to the bank."

"Well, you stop by and ask Cindy if she would like to have dinner with us tomorrow evening, okay?"

"It is a deal!"

Belle was beside herself thinking about Claire being engaged to Casey Anthony, their pastor! Knowing Claire, she had probably confessed her past to him, and he not only forgave her, but won't even remember it! Casey lived in the moment with much joy. Never had she met a kinder man, but Les Samuels did run a close second!

Belle mused, "I could fall in love with Les if I let myself go for just one moment."

Les had taken a special interest in Clay over the past few months. Clay was a natural with horses, and had already learned to run the barrels with one of Les' most promising quarter horses. Les said he was the youngest person he had ever seen master barrel racing, and mentioned going to an upcoming national rodeo event. Belle had a sudden "wake-up" call that she must protect Clay at all cost. He was an exceptional rider, and she did not want any publicity to surface that could place them at risk of being found. Just another reason that she could not get involved with Les. Just have to keep my guard up at all times! It may be time to move on. She was always contending with these mind battles, and lately they had all but consumed her. Sometimes, she even questioned her sanity when she would start to think about how Clay's dad was handling the loss of his wife and son.

"Stop it, don't think. Just got to stay busy and enjoy my sweet boy."

Clay came bouncing into the kitchen, and hollered, "Mom, we may go to Arizona next month!"

Belle stopped in her tracks, "What does Arizona have that Texas does not have?"

"A rodeo, Mom! And Mr. Samuels said I would be the youngest rider in history!"

"Darling, I've been thinking about doing a little traveling before you start to school, and we may not be here next month."

"I don't want to go anywhere, Mom. I would miss my horse and what about Dixie?"

"I tell you what, we'll think about our options and discuss it later, okay?"

Clay did not say another word. He walked out to the porch and sat in the swing.

Belle could tell he was more disturbed than she had ever witnessed. She joined him on the porch.

"May I sit in the swing with you, sweetheart?"

Clay grabbed her and held her tight. "I can't leave, Mom. I just can't do it. It hurts my heart too much!"

Belle held him and cried, too. No, she could not go through with this. There comes a point when you have to stop running, period. She was always running in her head. What kind of life was this going to be for Clay if she let their past destroy them both? She had run all kinds of risk trying to give him a good life, and she would continue! *Oh, Lord, let us live in the moment and give us Your peace that passeth all understanding.*

"Mom, my heart hurts so bad."

"Clay, Clay, son, we're not going anywhere. This is our home and this is where we'll stay, I promise."

That night Clay slept fitfully, and Belle realized how important stability was for his emotions. *Lord, I've got to turn all of this over to You. We are Your children and we must trust You for what is best in our lives. Please help me to be the mother that Clay needs, and Father, please help me to go forward in my life with Your Kingdom purpose as my priority. I ask You to forgive me for all my sins and protect and guard the heart of Clay's dad, dear Lord.*

—

It was their wedding day, and John could hardly wait to watch Anna walk down the aisle and become his wife! Every single detail had been taken care of by his sweet mom. How she loved Anna, the daughter she never had.

It seemed only yesterday that Anna was in a coma, and family and friends had rallied at the hospital and prayed for days, an unending vigil in hopes that God would give her a divine touch. John had fallen asleep with his head across her hospital bed, when he was awakened by Anna stroking his hair. When he looked into those beautiful blue eyes, he knew without a doubt God had answered their prayers, and he wanted this woman by his side for the rest of his life!

"Okay, there's the music, it is time to march on to another life!"

Anna was breathless just thinking about uniting with the man she loved with all her heart. She loved John in every way imaginable . . . body, mind, and spirit. She had felt for some time now that God brought them together for His purpose. Her recovery from her accident confirmed that they were destined to be one. When she first saw John after she came out of her coma, his eyes revealed that he loved her with a tenderness that she could never do without. And now, she was walking toward the man God intended for her to spend the rest of her life with. The church was full and the music carried her as though she were floating to the love of her life. Dreams do come true.

Esther's heart felt as though it would burst. She was so happy for her son, and could not be more thankful that he was marrying a woman like Anna. Anna was a "Proverbs" wife in every sense of the Word. Her joy was more than she could contain, and tears spilled down both cheeks . . . . tears of happiness and peace. Edmond glanced her way and leaned over and kissed her on the cheek.

Edmond wanted to take his wife in his arms and hold her forever. She was such a good woman. He was the man he was because of his Esther. He knew his son's life would have much healing because of Anna. John was a good man, but that Anna was such a mature Christian and sold out to God in all ways. She would be a wonderful wife for his son. John was radiant today and he looked years younger. Certainly, he still carried a heavy burden without his son, but Anna would be a healing balm. This was indeed a glorious day.

"And now I pronounce you man and wife. John, you may kiss your bride."

John kissed Anna and held her so close he was sure everyone could hear his heartbeat echoing throughout the church.

Anna felt that she had melted into his very soul.

Pastor Phillips announced, "I give you Mr. & Mrs. John Marshall!"

Everyone cheered and the organ music gave way to the wedding march as the whole church vibrated with celebration.

—

Al and Cindy had become sweethearts, and Al's life seemed to be filled with all things new. God had blessed him beyond his wildest dreams. Mr. Gibbs had mentioned that he wanted to retire early, and wished that Al would consider buying the hardware store. Al had talked it over with Mayme, and she knew God would work out every detail if it was His Will. He really wanted Cindy to be his wife, but at this point did not feel he could provide for his bride.

Al continued to restore Mayme's house and repair the fence that bordered her fifty-eight acres. It still seemed strange to him that Mayme never talked about her past . . . . just the present and always kept in mind God's Will for every conversation. She was a true saint and his angel. He could not begin to imagine where he would be right now if God had not worked through his humble vessel, Mayme.

As Al drove home from work that afternoon, something nagged at him. It was like an urgent nudge from the Holy Spirit. He dismissed going by Cindy's shop and decided to go straight home.

When Al pulled up in the driveway, he noticed that Mayme was not in her usual rocking chair on the front porch. Something clutched his heart, and he just knew that Mayme was in trouble! When he stepped inside the house, he saw her on the floor with her Bible beside her.

"Mayme, please be okay! Mayme, can you hear me?"

He gently took her up in his arms and laid her on the sofa. Slowly, her eyelids opened and her eyes searched his face.

"Dear God, in the precious Name of your Son, Jesus, I ask that you heal your precious servant, Mayme."

Mayme's eyes were bright and clear, but she did not move.

"Mayme, we're taking you to the hospital right now. You just hold on, I'm with you and I'll take care of everything."

—

Belle watched with her heart in her throat. It was always this way when Clay was running the barrels! Les had taught him well, and Clay was a natural, but she knew that there were certain risks regarding his safety. She was forever giving this to God and taking it back. Perhaps it was just a thing all parents did. She would always probably be too protective of her boy!

Belle jumped to her feet with a loud shout, "You won; you won!"

Clay had won many races with his favorite mare, Chico. She was a smaller horse, but fast as the wind, and Clay rode her as if he were part of her. It was always amazing to see how modest and shy he was during the trophy ceremonies. He had begun to win some handsome purses, too. At first all of his winnings went to Les Samuels, but now they split the winnings equally. Les had given Chico to Clay several weeks back, and told him he had won her fair and square. Les and Clay had become inseparable the last year.

Belle could not believe that Clay was six years old, and would start school in a few weeks. Her whole life was wrapped up in this precious little boy. Dixie had always remained loyal to Clay, too. She and Claire would on occasion ride with them to a rodeo, and Dixie would be the most avid cheerleader in support of her buddy, Clay. They would be attending the same school, and Clay had mentioned several times that he and Dixie could see one another every day. Belle felt good about Clay having a close friend that he could always share with. Belle never had a close friend growing up, and perhaps this was why she felt more comfortable with a little distance in her relationships.

"Hurry, Clay, we don't want to be late for the ceremony!"

"I'm coming, Mom. Will Dixie stay with us until Ms. Claire returns?"

"That's right. You guys are going to have more fun riding horses together, and sharing all your secrets!"

"Mom, how did you know I had secrets?"

Feeling totally caught off guard, Belle just laughed and said, "Everyone has at least one secret, sweetheart." She was hoping he might reveal a little more of his secrets.

"Mom, if I had an important secret, I would tell you," Clay smiled and grabbed her hand.

"I hope you know you can always come to me and tell me anything that is on your mind, especially things that concern you."

"I will, Mom, I promise."

When Belle and Clay arrived at the church, the first one to greet them was Les. He was all smiles. Pastor Anthony had asked Les to be his best man in the ceremony. Belle still found it hard to believe that Claire, her very best friend, would be marrying Pastor Casey Anthony. They were a great pair; both of them had servant's hearts. Pastor Anthony was one of the kindest men she had ever known. Belle was Claire's Matron of honor, and she felt nervous enough to be the bride.

"Okay, Clay, you and Dixie are on your honor. I'm going to the back of the church to be with Claire, and I want the two of you to be very quiet during the ceremony, okay? Dixie, this is your mom's special time, so you and Clay be very respectful."

"Promise, Ms. Belle, you can count on us! We can talk all we want later since I'll be staying a whole week with you!"

Les came by and touched her arm, "Let's go, it's time for the line up!"

Belle's heart skipped a beat when she heard the music start, and realized that some part of her wished that she were the one getting married.

—

Anna and John had a wonderful honeymoon discovering so many beautiful things about one another. Having a change of scenery brought about so much peace for them both. They each delighted in every moment of their time together. They both commented how their honeymoon had been a time of spiritual bonding, healing and beautiful love-making.

John had left for the office quite early this morning, so Anna was having a second cup of coffee and reading her morning devotional. For some reason her coffee had a metallic taste, and come to think of it, many of her favorite foods did not have their usual appeal. There was something else, too. She had not had a period since she and John were married. Just maybe, she could be pregnant. She and John had talked about taking some measures to prevent pregnancy for the first year or so, but decided to leave everything up to God's timing. For right now, she needed to get dressed and earn her keep. Dan had been taking up the slack at the office, and she could plainly see that he was over his head with paper work.

After John arrived at the office, he and Dan had discussed some of their ideas on expanding the office space and adding more personnel. God had blessed John and Dan's practice right out of their present real estate.

John now sat alone at his desk just reflecting on all of God's goodness. Anna was like a warm healing balm to his body and soul. He loved her more than life, and wanted more than anything to provide for her and protect her. One of the things he felt pretty strongly about was seeing her work part-time rather than full time. He hoped she would always be involved to some degree in his business. She knew the heartbeat of their practice, and both he and Dan felt Anna was their biggest asset. Above all she was very intuitive. That particular trait seemed to be absent from most men.

"Come on in, Anna. I was looking for you to come in later this morning. What's up?"

"John, it just hit me this morning. I could be pregnant!"

"Well, yes, you could. Are you saying you think you are?"

"Don't know, but think I'll make an appointment with my doctor to get a pregnancy test run."

"You are serious, aren't you? Anna, Anna, come here, darling."

He took her in his arms and held her so tenderly that she shuddered throughout her whole body.

—

Mayme could hear every word being spoken outside her room in the hallway. Dr. Boteler was making his recommendations to Al regarding the care she needed. Al was saying, no, he knew he could handle everything at home since their place was so close to his work. Mayme just smiled to herself . . . . their home. Yes, it was her home and Al's home, too. They were family, and she knew she could count on Al to help her through this time of rehabilitation. She had had a pretty debilitating stroke, but with Al's determination and help, she would get on her feet again . . . . she just had to.

Dr. Boteler covered Mayme's hand with his and said, "Well, Mayme, you have a pretty hard-headed young man here who insists that he is the one equipped to take care of you, and make sure you follow all of our instructions so your rehabilitation period will be minimal."

Al chimed in, "Mayme, we're taking you home first thing in the morning, and I'm guessing your recovery will be the fastest miracle Dr. Boteler has seen yet, especially after a week or so of eating my cooking!"

"Dr. Boteler, I've really never considered myself to be a chef, so Mayme will have to get well in self defense. She is the best cook ever. Just as soon as she is back in that kitchen, we'll have you over for some of her special fruit pie and tea."

"I can handle that."

Mayme could not speak or move her mouth, but those eyes of hers just danced. Al could tell she was so happy to be going home. She had been in the hospital and rehabilitation center for over a month now. She had gained most of her feeling back in her right side, but was still so weak that she could only get around with her walker. It really did not matter that she could not talk yet, certainly that would come later. What a blessing it was to be able to move about with her walker.

"Mayme, I'm going to head out to the store, but will be back at noon, okay?"

"Dr. Boteler, I'll see you in the morning when you discharge Mayme. Promise, I'll be the best nurse she could have. You'll see."

"You know, Al, love goes a long way towards any recovery. I'm confident you and Mayme will be a winning combination!"

Al and Cindy went to Cindy's house after the two of them visited Mayme that evening. Cindy could sense that Al had something on his mind, but just remained quiet until he wanted to share. They had eaten leftovers with little conversation passing between them.

"Cindy, I've been thinking about how I can best take care of Mayme during these next few weeks when her rehab is so needful. I was wondering if you would consider taking a two hour break from your shop around noon and preparing Mayme a bite to eat and just visiting with her. Maybe you could get her out on the porch for a little sunshine, and just let her know that you really want to be with her. I could take an hour off mid morning and then again mid afternoon to help her with her exercises. And of course, I would be able to fix breakfast and dinner for her. I don't know, Cindy. Am I asking too much from you?"

Cindy threw her head back and laughed in that usual uninhibited way. "Al, I cannot think of anything I would rather do then help you and Mayme. You two are the love of my life! I would do anything for either of you. It will be an honor to visit with Mayme at lunch time and prepare a nice meal for us. I probably need to take more time away from the shop, anyway. Come to think of it, rarely do I have customers until after 2:00 in the afternoon. Absolutely, count me in!"

Cindy could see the relief in Al's face, and what a handsome face he had. She had observed during the last few months how tenderly he treated Mayme, and she found that she had fallen in love with him because he had so much love to give. The first time they kissed, Cindy had initiated it, and in that first kiss, she knew this was the man God had hand-picked for her. She never had to initiate another kiss. He was so tender and sweet with his affection, and never once had he been anything but a true gentleman in all respects.

"Cindy, certainly you must know how I feel about you."

"I'd like to hear you tell me."

"I see, you're going to make this difficult for me!" he said with a chuckle.

"I need for you to be a man of more words at times, Al . . . you know that."

"As Mayme would say, sometimes more is less."

"I know you don't talk about your past much, and perhaps there are some things you may not be particularly proud of, but there is not a single person who has not made their share of mistakes. Our relationship has been based on our love for Jesus and others. We aren't supposed to dwell on our past mistakes or wrong choices when we've been made a new creature in Christ. Let's just always be honest with one another from this point forward, and God will take care of the rest."

"Cindy, I want more than anything to live in the present and aspire for a future with you walking hand in hand with God, but I also want to be honest with you about some things in my past that may or may not affect our lives in the future."

"Al, when you start talking "ifs" I'm not sure we're trusting God. You know He indeed has the plan for our lives, and I don't think we are to doubt for one moment. I'm perfectly willing to walk with you one day at a time. God gives us grace for twenty-four hours at the time. Are we going to receive His grace and trust or do we choose to go the world's way and be anxious or even afraid? Honestly, Al, I don't want to go the world's way. Let's trust God for each day, okay? All we have is just today, Al."

"You make it all sound so easy."

"We have choices, Al, and I choose you from this day forward."

"I guess I best ask you to marry me before we walk down the aisle, right? My sweet Cindy, will you be my wife for the rest of our lives?"

"Yes, I will be your wife. Thought you'd never ask!"

"I know someone who will be so happy about this news. Matter of fact it might be just what she needs to motivate her to stick to this rehab program. Cindy, you are such a love for helping me with Mayme. You know we'll have to wait until she is well enough to enjoy our wedding. What do you think about three or four months from now?"

"A fall wedding sounds perfect! Perhaps we can have the ceremony outside. Would you be in favor?"

"You plan the details and I'll show up. Let's just watch our budget, okay?"

"Al, we'll work together on that part. You are an excellent money manager, so I'll need your guidance."

"Okay, sweet Cindy. Walk me to the truck. Got to get my beauty rest tonight. Mayme and I have a big day tomorrow. I'm going to take off for the morning. I think Stan can handle the store by himself. Mayme will be my number one priority tomorrow!"

"Al, it just amazes me how loving and tender you are with Mayme. I've never witnessed anyone care for their own mother like you do Mayme. You are genuine to the bone marrow, do you know that?"

"I know someone who is prejudiced!" Al said as he gave Cindy a hug before leaving.

—

Belle was excited about the Christmas Eve party that Claire and Casey were hosting. She had baked a couple of cakes and also made Clay's favorite chocolate pie. It was time to check in on Clay and Dixie and head on out to the party.

"Okay kids, it is time to collect the gifts. Grab your jackets and Clay, would you take one of these cakes to the car for me? Please be careful. I'll open the door for you two."

"Ms. Belle, thank you so much for letting us help you in the kitchen today, and we didn't make a mess, either! I think I could bake a cake by myself, now."

"Dixie, I want you to make me a chocolate cake. I love chocolate, don't I, Mom?"

"You are not alone. I think everyone loves chocolate, even Barney, although you know we should not feed him much because chocolate is not good for a dog."

"I'll never give him any more chocolate. He is my buddy and I don't want him to be sick. Dixie, don't ever feed Barney chocolate, okay?"

"I would never do anything to hurt Barney. He is the sweetest dog ever!"

"Mom, Barney will live a long time, won't he?"

"Yes, darling. You take very good care of him, and I'm sure he'll be with us a very long time. Okay, you two, let's not be so serious. We're going to be joyful and thankful that we can celebrate Jesus' birthday. We have so many blessings and wonderful friends. And Dixie, you are going to have a baby sister or brother in just four more months! Are you excited?"

"I'm so very excited, Ms. Belle. Are you going to have a baby soon, too, so Clay can have a brother or sister?"

"First things first, and that would be getting married to the man God chooses for me."

Clay piped up like a little canary. "I know who that is! It is Mr. Les. I know he cares a lot for you, Mom, and he would be a good daddy for me, too!"

Belle could not believe how having conversations with little people could bring things to light so fast. They say exactly what's on their minds at all times . . . . just amazing. The thoughts she would not allow herself to have, Clay verbalized with such honesty and freedom. Her sweet little boy was so pure and honest.

April 2000

Belle was drowning in pain so intense she could not think. She wanted to throw up, faint and die all at once! Dr. Moore had discouraged a natural birth, but Belle would not listen to his advice. She was determined to do nothing whatsoever that could affect her baby's healthy start in life. If she could only focus on Les' confident expression and that big smile of his. This too shall pass . . . . it has to.

"Belle, we need one more hard and long push. Come on, you can do it!"

Les held her hand firmly and smiled.

Belle heard herself cry out and immediately, she heard someone else's small cry. Then that little whimper turned into a siren. "Oh, God, my baby . . . . my very own baby!"

"Sweetheart, we have a tiny little girl and she is beautiful!"

Les was crying and kissing Belle's face lightly all over.

Dr. Moore announced, "Mr. and Mrs. Samuels, may I present to you a very healthy beautiful baby girl!"

Belle's heart and emotions had never known such ecstasy in her entire life. With Les's arms wrapped around her and their baby enclosed between them, surely her heart would burst!

Dear Lord, please let me treasure this moment for the rest of my life and never let one ounce of intensity slip through my memory.

Les bounced out of the delivery room and burst into the waiting room leaping and laughing. He went straight to Clay and assured him that his mother was fine and he had a new baby sister.

Clay was so relieved he started crying, and of course Dixie was right beside him comforting him and laughing at the same time.

Dixie jumped up and down. "It's a girl, it's a girl, yea, I'm so happy! Just think, Clay, I have a younger brother and now you've got a younger sister! What a fine day. I can't wait to tell Mom! I'll be right back after I give her a call!"

Dixie went down the hall to use the payphone to call her mother.

"Mom, we have a girl and everything is fine!"

"What marvelous news. Aren't we blessed?" Claire said.

Clay strolled by Dixie waving and signaling his departure for the house.

His baby sister's arrival was just in the nick of time. He had one day to prepare for the national rodeo events, which were 200 miles away. He hoped that his parents would let him drive the distance by himself. He had been driving their truck for only a couple of months and had pulled the horse trailer once with his dad in the passenger's seat. He would love to take Dixie with him for moral support, but had not felt at liberty to ask her parents because of an overnight stay. Pastor Casey was really strict with Dixie and Clay could certainly appreciate her dad being protective. Dixie was the most beautiful girl he had ever seen, and everyone in the community thought so highly of her. Actually, it seemed that she was everybody's girl and they all took an interest in her.

Clay had placed Belle's Boy in the stall early that morning. He was an amazing horse in every respect. They had purchased him when he was two, and he quickly grew to be everyone's pet. His mom had called him her big boy and would hand feed him often. He became so attached to his mom that the name Belle's Boy seemed to fit the big guy. Of all the horses Clay had ridden in barrel races, Belle's Boy was the biggest. Boy was a fine looking horse. He was a buckskin with black stockings and black mane and tail.

"Hey Boy, are you ready to roll? We've got an exciting time ahead of us tomorrow. If we win this one, I'll have plenty saved up for my college funds!"

"Hi guys!"

"Dixie, you startled me!"

"I'd say we've had plenty of excitement today, wouldn't you? Have you talked to your folks about driving by yourself to Wichita Falls tomorrow?"

"No. What I've been thinking about is perhaps asking your folks if they would allow you to go with me, and that would increase my chances of my parents giving me permission to pull the trailer. Even when dad drives, he always likes for me to stay alert and watch for things he may miss. What do you think?"

"Gosh, Clay, I don't know that my parents would give me approval especially since it would mean staying over for the night. I just don't think so."

"Do you think it would offend them for me to at least ask?"

"Of course not. We'll go together and talk with them, okay?"

"Thanks, Dixie."

Casey was preparing his sermon in his study when Dixie and Clay entered.

"Hi kids, what's up?"

Dixie looked at him with the purest and most honest look. "Dad, Clay and I have something we want to discuss with you."

"Sure!"

"Clay would like for me to ride with him to Wichita Falls for the national rodeo events. Actually, we do not know yet if his parents will allow him to go because he has only pulled the trailer on one occasion, but with my help in the passenger's seat, his parents might give their consent."

"Pastor Casey, I would take care of Dixie's hotel expense and pay for all of her food as well."

"I'm sure this rodeo event means a lot to you, Clay, for you to ask me to consider letting Dixie travel with you. You'll have to give me a few hours to pray about this and talk it over with Claire. I know the two of you are responsible and capable of making such a trip, but I need God's discernment, so let's talk again this evening, okay?"

"Yes sir, Pastor Casey. Thanks for considering my request."

The two departed for the stables to prepare for their trip in hopes their parents would give their consents.

"Hey, Dixie, I've got an idea. Let's get everything packed up in the trailer, and then go up to the house and see what we can fix up in the kitchen for Dad to eat when he gets home from the hospital. Also, I want to go by the little flower shop on Main and pick up an arrangement for Mom. We have to go back and see my little sister this afternoon!"

"I find it so hard to believe that you have a baby sister! You'll be an extra protective older brother, I'm sure!"

"I'll protect her just like I protect you, Dixie! I would fight for you in a second!"

"Well, I'm pretty independent, you know. Don't think you have to worry about me!"

—

Belle looked down into the sweet and pure face of her newborn daughter, and prayed that this child would have a blessed life and one that God's purpose would evidence in every way.

"Okay my beautiful Belle, what are we going to name our precious gift from God?"

I've been thinking about a befitting name for some time now, and since she has arrived, I think Rebecca Laura sounds nice, and we could call her Laura. What are your thoughts, Les?"

Les bent down and kissed Belle on the forehead and said, "Laura is perfect in every way, my sweet wife."

Clay gently knocked on his mom's door before entering with a large bouquet of freshly cut flowers. "Congratulations, Mom!"

"Oh, my darling boy, you think of everything, don't you?"

"No, of course not."

"Darling, you just missed seeing your little sister. We've had her here for the last couple of hours, but now she is back in the nursery room down the way. Why don't you go see her! Oh, yes, her name is Laura. What do you think?"

"Oh, Mom, it is a beautiful name. A name you would think of, right Dad?"

"Yep, son, you are on the money! You know your mom!"

Belle's heart had never been so full of love. She had the most wonderful children a mother could ever hope for.

"Mom, Dad, I have something I really need to discuss with you, and I don't want to take away any of your joy with baby Laura, but this is pretty important to me, and I would like for you to consider my request."

"Anything, Clay, what is it, darling?"

"You know the rodeo events start tomorrow evening in Wichita Falls, and Dad, I know the last thing you want to do right now is leave Mom and Laura. Would you and Mom give me your permission to travel to this event? I know your feelings about having an extra person to keep a watchful eye on the horse trailer, so I have asked Dixie's parents if they would allow her to go with me. And Mom, one more thing, if this would keep you in a state of worry, then I'll pass on the event."

Les placed his arm on Clay's shoulder and pulled him close. "We realize that this is your biggest event of the year, so your mom and I will discuss your wishes and let you know of our decision by this evening. Why don't you go see that little sister of yours, now!"

After Clay walked out, Belle let out a little sigh.

"Les, I cannot imagine Casey letting Dixie go with Clay when it is just the two of them."

"Why, Belle?"

"You know as well as I do that those two are so close, and I would hate to think we opened a door of temptation for them."

"You, know, Belle, they have plenty of chances right here in town all the time for hormones to get out of control. And another thing, we really don't have any choice, but to trust our children. What more can we do at this point? We've tried to place family focus on God first, and Belle, that is the best we've got going for us. It will have to be up to the leadership of the Holy Spirit regarding choices of both of these young adults. Don't you agree?"

"I suppose. So, do you think we should give our consent for him to go, if indeed, Casey and Claire allow Dixie to go?"

"Sweetheart, this is how I see things. If Dixie is allowed to go then let's give Clay our permission, but if Dixie doesn't go, I'd rather Clay did not haul the trailer alone. Perhaps we need to let the deciding factor rest with the decision of Casey and Claire, okay?"

"Agreed. You're right, Les. That is a good judgment call."

Les walked in the house, and headed straight to the kitchen. He had forgotten about eating, and now it was dinner time, and his appetite was enormous. He could smell something divine coming from the kitchen the minute he walked into the house.

"Hey, Dad! I bet you are surprised to see your supper cooked!"

"Speechless is more like it. Just how did I rate anything other than leftovers?"

"Maybe I thought it might encourage you to say "yes" to the nationals tomorrow night!"

"Clay, has anyone ever told you how totally honest you always are?"

"Not really, but Dad, I always have uppermost in my mind that the truth sets us free."

"So true, son."

"Well, where is Dixie and have her folks given her permission to go on the trip?"

"Pastor Casey is still praying about all of this, and Dixie is staying with Elliott while Claire goes to visit Mom and Laura."

"Did you and Mom discuss my pulling the trailer without you?"

"No, we didn't get into those details, not to dismiss the fact that safety is vital, but your mom and I decided if Casey and Claire gave Dixie permission, then we would give you ours."

"And what if they don't let Dixie go?"

"You stay, Clay."

"Okay, Dad, I can accept that and I thank you for placing your trust in my judgment calls. You and Mom are the greatest parents in the world, but I'm sure you already know that!"

"It always feels good to hear those words, though!"

—

Dixie and Elliott were playing a board game when their dad came out of his study.

"Dixie, your mom and I discussed your making this trip with Clay. She thought since it seemed that Clay would not be able to go unless you accompanied him that we should give you our permission. I've prayed long about this, and I have to admit I have some reservations, which do not directly concern you, but how this could look to some of the members of our congregation, especially some who wag their tongues. Placing that aside, though, I agree with your mom, so we're giving you our permission."

"Dad, thanks so much. You know I'll be responsible and safe."

"Yes, Dixie, I do know, and it is a comfort to have a teenager who has such a level head. I will be praying for your safety, and you must give us a call when you arrive, okay?"

"Yes sir. Thank you so much, Dad. This will mean so much to Clay."

Dixie drove over to the stables where she found Clay cleaning Boy's gear. She ran up behind him and placed her fingers over his eyes.

"You'll never guess, not in a million years!"

"Dixie, you are being silly. Who else sneaks upon me, but you!"

"I meant guess 'what' not who?"

Clay's eyes widened and he gave her one of his mile wide smiles. "Your parents are letting you go to nationals with me!"

"Yes!"

"And you know what else? My folks said if you were allowed to go, then I had their permission. Come on girl, we have a lot to pack up!"

Clay was up at 4:00 a.m. loading all of Boy's gear, food, extra shoes, just in case he threw one, plus the outfit he planned to wear that night for the evening event. His stomach was churning. There were so many things going round and round in his mind . . . his new baby sister, the responsibility of hauling the trailer, the possibility of winning $10,000 tonight should he place first. The thoughts just raced on and on.

He wanted to go by the hospital on his way to pick up Dixie, and give his mom a kiss and look in on sweet, beautiful Laura. What a blessing to have a little sister. He was already thinking about teaching her to ride just as soon as she could walk!

Clay loaded up Boy, secured the trailer door, hopped in the truck, bowed his head and said a prayer. He knew he had an awesome responsibility, and he also knew his limitations, but what he knew beyond a shadow of a doubt was that God was able.

By the time he picked up Dixie it was 8:00. He hoped to be in Wichita Falls no later than 2:00.

"I brought some sandwiches and fruit. I bet you haven't taken the time to even eat breakfast, have you?"

"Actually, I haven't. Would you hand me half of a sandwich, please? Sorry, I did not get to express my appreciation to your folks, but I will when we return."

"Clay, they understand about the need to get on the road early, and besides, we'll have some great news to share with them when we do get back, right?"

"And just what would that be, dear Dixie?"

"I know you and Boy are going to get first place tonight, I just know it!"

"What's to be, will be."

"Clay, you always say that. Are you aware that is pretty much your take on how everything goes?"

"No, Dixie, I never thought about it."

"You know, Clay, just lately, I've noticed that you seem preoccupied at times, not a lot, but some. Now, what is that all about? What have you been pondering?"

"Leave it to you to notice every little thing!"

"I'm serious, Clay. Have you reached the age that you are not going to share everything with me?"

"Of course not, Dixie. That is ridiculous!"

"Well, share, then."

"You are very perceptive, and truth be known, I have had some odd feelings since Barney died a couple of years ago. And lately, I've had some disturbing dreams. I know this will sound weird, but I've felt somewhat disconnected since Barney is no longer with us."

"Well, why are you just now telling me about this, Clay?"

"I guess because I don't know how to connect the dots enough to tell anyone."

"Well, I'm always here for you whenever you want to talk, but you know I'm not going to pry into your personal thoughts."

"I really like that about you, Dixie. You have an uncanny ability to respect another's space."

"You know what I've been thinking about lately?"

"It is no telling . . . . what?"

"I will probably be leaving for Brown University in less than six months, and that is miles and miles from here."

"You don't know yet if you'll get a scholarship."

"I've got that gut feeling, and if I get it, you know I need to take advantage of it. My folks have been so faithful to promote my interest in journalism, and give me every study tool to insure that I'll have opportunities that they did not have."

"Wow, I guess I'll have to keep up my grades, so I can come join you after I graduate."

"Just think about it Clay, we've never been apart."

"Yea, I've had a few thoughts lately about that very thing."

"Have you thought about what you want to do in life as far as a profession?"

"Man, yea, I'm going to be a rodeo guy!"

"No, Clay, this is only for a season, and you know that!"

"Honestly, the only thing that always comes to mind, is going into the ministry."

"Really?"

"Started having these thoughts about the time Barney died."

"Hmmm. That's interesting."

"Hey, I'm only sixteen . . . a lot I know!"

"A calling is a calling regardless of what your age. Do you feel you are called to preach?"

"Maybe. Just not sure . . . . what's to be, will be."

"Right. Yes, that's the perfect answer!"

"How about turning around and making sure Boy is settled in well."

"All is well."

"By the way, thanks for coming with me, Dixie. I really do not know what I would do without you."

"I wouldn't have missed it for the world!"

The two of them settled into a comfortable banter, and before they knew it, the large banner to the rodeo arena and stables was in full view.

"I need to give my folks a call to let them know we've safely arrived. I'll ask them to call your parents for us, okay?"

"Hey, that would be great. Thanks, Dixie."

Dixie left to find a pay phone in the area where all the exhibitors displayed their products. She was getting caught up in all the excitement of competition, plus the aroma of hamburgers, fries and popcorn. The smells were that of a fair. She and Clay had always gone to the fair together. Actually, they had always done just about everything together. For the very first time, she thought about how much she cared for Clay, really cared. She viewed herself as fiercely independent, except where it came to

Clay. In some ways she wanted to protect him, but of course that was silly. He was a strong man already. He was at least six feet, and had the most gorgeous blonde hair and huge brown eyes. She had begun to notice this past summer how all the girls stared at him.

Searching for the correct change in her pocket, she picked up the phone, and dialed her parents.

"Hey Mom, we made it."

"Praise God, it is so good to hear your voice and know the two of you are safe."

"Everything will be just fine, Mom, so please don't worry. I'll give you a call when we are leaving to come home tomorrow, okay?"

"Thanks, Sweetie. Take care and I love you."

"I love you, too, Mom. Bye for now. Oh, wait, hey Mom, would you give Clay's parents a call?"

"Sure, right now. Bye."

Dixie walked back over to the stables and spotted Boy right away. He was in one of the front stalls closest to the performance circle. Everyone that passed by wanted to touch him, ask questions about his past performances and how quickly he could run the barrels. He was such a handsome horse, and for the most part just a big pet. The only time you would see him jumpy or excited was just seconds before he entered the arena for his barrel race. Other than that, he was gentle as a lamb. Come to think of it, Clay was a lot like Boy! Suddenly, Dixie realized she was having way too many thoughts of Clay, and in a different way than she had viewed him before. Her thoughts were unsettling to say the least.

"Hey Dixie, guess what our number is tonight?"

"I have no idea, what is it?"

"It is God's number, SEVEN!"

"Great, that's a good sign you'll win!"

"Can you believe we only have an hour left before competition begins?"

"Yea, I know. I'm going to find me the best seat in the house!"

"Not until I get my good luck hug."

"Well, of course."

She hugged him and silently said a prayer, knowing he was doing the same.

"See you at intermission, okay?"

"Right."

As Dixie settled into a front row seat where she had a clear view of the barrel racing, her thoughts about Clay were like a stampede in her head. Why, all of a sudden, was she beginning to think about the future instead of just enjoying the moment? Their childhood together had come to an abrupt halt, and every thought seemed to be jumping ahead into unknowns regarding their future. Why should it matter so much? She had six more months with her best friend and what she had been comfortable with for most of her life. *Dear God, settle me into the peace of Jesus, let me live the moment to the fullest, looking to You and You alone for my every need.*

"Hi there, mind if I sit here?"

"Fine, I'm not saving any seats."

"My name is Laris Scott. I'm a reporter for the Daily Herald."

"Nice to meet you, my name is Dixie Anthony."

"Ms. Anthony, I've been interested in a young man named Clay Samuels for quite a while, and attended barrel races that he placed well in. Do you happen to know who I'm talking about?"

"Actually, he is a good friend of mine. We live in the same community."

"I'm hoping he'll be the grand prize winner tonight. I really want to do an article on him."

"You know, Mr. Scott, Clay has always been extremely private and avoided any type of publicity in past events. He is a very modest person, and would be most uncomfortable being the center of attention."

"He has somewhat been labeled the "Ghost Rider" in my circles. We've tried to talk with him in past events, and somehow he always escapes us. He is a real challenge, I can tell you that!"

"Mr. Scott, you are certainly welcomed to view all the events here beside me, but I don't feel comfortable discussing Clay's life, okay?"

"Okay, Ms. Anthony, end of discussion. I'm going to walk down to the concession stand, and I would like to leave my camera here, if you don't mind."

"That's fine with me."

The seats looked to be completely filled. It was a sellout tonight, and she was beginning to get a bit nervous. She always felt anxious right before Clay rode. She really had mixed emotions . . . wanting him to win, of course, but not wanting him to get hurt, either. So Clay was known as the "Ghost Rider." Wonder how long the newspaper folks have followed Clay. He was really well-known by all of the rodeo circuits. In the southwestern rodeo circles, Clay had been a child star. By the time he was ten years old, he could run the barrels faster than anyone. Seems like there was a particular write-up in the newspapers when he was twelve that Ms. Belle had gotten quite upset over, and since then Clay had kept a very low profile regarding the news media. Truly, they were the most private people she knew.

"I brought you some popcorn!"

"Thanks, Mr. Scott!"

"Here we go, and the first competition is the barrels!"

"Yes, there are two barrel races for each contestant, and the person who has the top score from both wins the grand prize, $10,000."

"That's a nice purse tonight. I know you must be really excited for your friend!"

"Yes, I am. If he should win, he'll have saved enough to pay for his college education!"

"I see."

Both sat in silence for the first six contestants. Dixie could see Clay and Boy right behind the arena opening. Clay was calm and composed, as always, but Boy had that anticipated win in his eyes, as he danced from side to side.

Dixie was on her feet screaming, "Go Boy, go Boy, you can do it!"

"What a perfect ride! Listen to that score, just unbelievable! Hey, Dixie, isn't that some kind of record?"

"Not sure, but it is the best score Clay has had yet!"

The crowd was screaming and rooting for their star. Finally, everyone was seated and the barrel racing continued. The night was still young. There were many different types of competition, and the second barrel event would be the night's finale.

Clay walked up to where Dixie was seated. He was wearing that beautiful smile of his, and his eyes were dancing!

Dixie stood up, took his hand, and introduced him to Laris Scott.

"Hello, Mr. Scott."

"Nice riding, Clay, matter of fact, you are the best!"

"It is all in the horse, Mr. Scott."

"Clay, I wonder if you would be open for an interview after the last event tonight?"

"Thank you, sir, but I don't think so. Please excuse us; we're going to the stables. Dixie, shall we?"

Dixie caught his hand, and followed as they weaved their way through the mass of people.

"Clay, if you win, what would be the harm in talking to Mr. Scott? He seemed nice enough."

"Dixie, I'm really not sure why I feel uncomfortable except for the fact I always want to protect our privacy. Probably something Mom instilled in me years ago. She has always been a little over protective when it came to me . . . . not sure why. Shall we grab a bite to eat? There is at least another hour before the barrel competition starts up again."

"Sounds great to me!"

As the two stood in line to order their food, Dixie noticed that Mr. Scott was ahead of them. She hoped there would not be another awkward encounter since Clay felt uncomfortable talking with Mr. Scott.

"Clay, I'll have a hamburger and coke."

"We would like to order two hamburgers, two cokes and a large order of French fries, please."

The man behind the counter said, "Hope you enjoy. Your meal has already been paid by the gentleman, who just left to go back into the arena, and he sure left a nice tip, too."

"Oh, Clay, I bet that was Mr. Scott!"

"That was really nice of him. Sure hope I don't have to pay up in the future!"

"Actually, he didn't seem that forward to me. Let's give him the benefit of the doubt!"

The two walked over to an empty table to sit and enjoy their food. Clay was quiet, so Dixie took her cue and kept her thoughts to herself. She was just dying to ask him how he felt about the possibility of winning the grand prize, but knew in her heart these things could be discussed later when they were on their way home. *Oh, dear Lord, if it is Your Will, please let Clay win the next event. These funds will help him to be more independent, and I believe he needs this right now, since his mom has a new baby and won't have as much time for him. Thank you, Lord.*

The announcer blared over the loud speaker that the last event of the season would be starting in fifteen minutes!

"That's us, Dixie!"

"Oh, Clay, my heart is thudding in my chest! I seem to get overly caught up in these events, and I know in my heart of hearts it is because I want God's very best for you. I know how much this means to you, and I want all your dreams to come true, Clay!"

"Be peaceful, Dixie . . . what's to be, is to be . . . just enjoy the journey, and I'm going to enjoy the ride!"

"You are always so wise, Clay. Okay, I'm headed back to my winning seat! God go with you."

As they departed, Dixie realized all at once that she was in love with Clay Samuels. Oh, my, she had so many new emotions to surface. She could have shouted this revelation to the world!

Mr. Scott stood while she slid past to take her seat. He smiled with a nod, but did not strike up a conversation. She had to admit, she really wanted to remain quiet and ponder in her head what was going on in her heart.

Clay's turn was next. The rider before had an excellent score to be combined with his first race and was nicely lined up to take the purse. If anything happened to slow Boy's stride, then Clay would not win. Dixie forced all negatives to the back of her mind, and said a prayer to claim Clay the winner and God the victor!

On her feet cheering Clay and Boy on, Dixie realized that Mr. Scott was doing the same. At the end of the race, Clay was declared winner of the annual national rodeo event, and Dixie and Laris Scott embraced in their excitement!

"Oh, Mr. Scott, thanks so much for treating us to supper!"

"Wow, how can you think of such a small detail at a time like this?"

"Please, come with me to congratulate Clay, okay?"

"Don't want to spoil the moment, Dixie."

"I really don't think you will . . . please do come."

"You first, let's go down and see our Ghost Rider!"

Clay was covered up in well-wishers, so Dixie and Laris observed in the background until Clay caught sight of Dixie. They embraced and expressed their enthusiasm genuinely to one another. Laris snapped a few pictures as did everyone else. The announcer was asking for Clay to come up to the podium and accept the prize and say a few words to all the fans and contestants.

After being congratulated and accepting the large trophy and money, Clay took the microphone, softly cleared his throat, and began speaking. "I am humbled that so many wonderful people have made an investment of time mostly, but certainly money, too, so that I can stand here and be honored. I'm sure I do not fully comprehend the sacrifices my parents have made for me to have this opportunity, but I thank them and God from the bottom of my heart. And not to forget . . . my very best friend is here with me tonight, and if it were not for her, I would not have been a contestant! Thanks, everyone."

Oh, how proud she was of him. He was so honest, unselfish and a humble servant of God. How her heart felt it would burst!

As he walked away from the podium, the crowd continued to applaud. It seemed that he was everyone's hero, but most of all he was her hero!

It was past midnight and Dixie was still wide awake. She and Clay had not really had much time to reflect over his victory. He was totally exhausted and after getting Boy settled in the stall with food and water, they had come straight to the hotel and gone to their individual rooms, which were side by side. Clay had helped her with her bag, bid her goodnight and closed the door between their rooms. She could not remember Clay being so quiet as he was after the event. It was unsettling to her, even though she knew he was in need of sleep. She could not put her finger on it, but something was troubling him.

As Dixie was just dropping off to sleep, she heard a muffled cry! And again, then followed by crying. "Could it be Clay?"

She jumped out of bed, and knocked on the door between them. There was no answer, so she turned on the light and opened the door.

"Dixie, is that you?"

"Yes, Clay, are you alright?"

"I am so sorry I awakened you, Dixie."

"It is okay. You must have had a bad dream."

"I'll say. Actually, it is a recurring dream, and it always seems so real."

"Do you want to tell me about it?"

She sat down on the bed beside him, and could feel him shivering.

"I don't think I want to talk about it right now, but please stay a few minutes."

"Clay, lie back down and let me cover you up, you are shaking. I'll stay beside you on top of the cover until you get back to sleep, okay?"

"Thanks, Dixie."

There was a little light shining from her room, but not enough to keep Clay awake, so she just placed her arm around him and held him close until he quit trembling and dozed off to sleep.

There seemed to be such a heaviness that came over her and when the light of morning shone through the blinds, she found herself wrapped in Clay's strong arms as he continued to slumber.

Yes, it had been a perfectly harmless night, but it seemed in the last twenty-four hours, there had been light years of intensity added to their already strong emotional bond. She released herself from Clay's arms, slipped out of the bed, and tiptoed to her room.

She took a shower and got dressed. As she was getting her bag packed and closed, she heard the truck door slam, and knew Clay was anxious to go load up Boy and get on the road.

"Good morning, Dixie! Are you ready for some breakfast?"

"Absolutely, thought you'd never ask!"

"We'll load up Boy, and stop by that little diner on the outskirts of town before we head home."

"Wonderful!"

During the time Boy was being loaded and their drive to the diner, Clay was extremely quiet. He seemed very preoccupied. Before entering the diner, Dixie caught sight of a newspaper with Clay's picture on the front.

"Hey, I want to purchase the newspaper, okay?"

"Sure, we'll take a look at the rodeo article while we eat."

"Wow, Clay, your picture is on the front page! It was bound to happen. I bet that Mr. Scott wrote something about you. Let's have a look!"

After reading the article, she handed the front page to Clay. "Read it for yourself. It is a nice write up and very professional."

"No more Mr. Elusive Ghost Rider. I have finally been exposed. There are no more secrets!"

"Well, you have to admit, you've been so modest, it has almost seemed that you were being secretive."

"Maybe."

"Clay, what was last night all about? The terrible dream you had and such extreme reactions."

"I wish I knew. It is the strangest thing how this came about after Barney died. At first I just figured it was a form of grief and anxieties, but the dreams continue and are so vivid!"

"Can you share them with me?"

"It seems dreadful to talk about such, Dixie. The dreams are so morbid. Maybe I'll share another time when things aren't so fresh. I just want to forget it."

"Sure, Clay, but you have to know I'm always here for you."

"Oh, I do know that. You stayed with me all night."

"Clay, I really did not mean to fall asleep, but I did."

"Thanks for staying. I needed the peaceful sleep."

"So this happens frequently and interrupts your sleep?"

"Lately, yes."

"Have you talked with your folks about it?"

"No, and I don't feel comfortable sharing with them. They have a new life with little Laura, and don't need extra duty where I'm concerned. After all, I need to be responsible for myself. I'll be making my own way soon enough."

"Sometimes, I can hardly bear the fact that you and I are approaching adulthood, and will have totally separate lives soon."

"Dixie, let's not go there. Please let's just live the moment and enjoy our youth."

"Marvelous idea. I've had way too much seriousness whirling around in my little mind lately. What about two chocolate malts for the road? I'll buy!"

"Deal!"

It was the twins' thirteenth birthday, and Esther and Edmond were throwing them their first surprise party at the Country Club. Anna was to work out the details of getting them there without revealing the reason.

"Edmond, can you believe our grandchildren are thirteen years old? Where have the years gone?"

"Well, they are certainly not etched in your beautiful face because you haven't aged one bit since the day I met you!"

"Nor you, my sweet husband."

"Neither of us sees that well anymore, right?"

They laughed and kissed as Esther continued to wrap birthday gifts for her precious Allie and Alan. Both were angels straight from God, as was their mother. Anna had been the one constant in her son's life since Kate's death and Eddie's disappearance. As she went back down memory lane, she remembered the day of the wedding, and feeling that John's life had a new beginning, and one that would bless him until the day he died.

There were still times when Esther could see the terrific void in John's heart over losing Eddie. Maybe not the loss so much as the unknowns surrounding his disappearance. Not any of them had closure, but through God's mercy and grace there had been a gradual acceptance. Esther still knew in her heart of hearts that Eddie was somewhere and that God was watching over him. God had given her the peace of Jesus. And since the birth of the twins, life had been so rich and full. She thanked God every day for restoring to her family what the locust had eaten. God was so good.

John was still at the office finishing up some last minute details on a case he was helping Dan with. Oh, what excitement this evening would harvest with the surprise party for his children. This was the first surprise party they had ever planned, so there was excitement in the air for all involved in the scheming!

As John reflected on the lives of these two precious gifts from God, he could not help thinking about Eddie. Where could he be? What was he doing or was he even alive? Let's see, he would be almost seventeen. Wow, where had the years gone! *Oh, God, it only matters that he is okay, and if he is, please in Your timing bring him back into our lives.* He and Anna had told the twins about Eddie's disappearance when they were old enough to comprehend. They felt it better for them to know the truth from their parents, than to hear bits and pieces through the children of parents who may have remembered the incident.

He was so proud of Allie and Alan. They were twins, but their interests and behavior could not be more opposite. Allie was studious and loved to read, especially her Bible. Alan was all boy! He loved horses, sports and girls! Alan had been riding various horses at some boarding stables for people who did not have time to ride their horses and keep them in shape. His real love was going to the rodeos and trying to follow his hero, the Ghost Rider. He had talked non-stop after seeing a recent write-up in the paper about his hero. Apparently, this kid had been riding in the rodeo circuits since he was six or so. Just watching both of his children come into their own was absolutely fascinating. He and Anna encouraged them both to stay involved in church and community service. To Allie, this was her fondest dream, but to Alan, nothing could be further . . . such opposites!

Anna was his true love. He loved her with a passion, admired her, depended on her wisdom and more than anything wanted to provide for her and take care of her for a lifetime. She still worked part-time for the law firm. She kept the auditors challenged at all times. No one could keep books as accurately as Anna. She was just a natural at so many things. She did not know what it was to say "no" to anyone, but the children on occasion. She was a wise and Godly mother, and his kids shined because of her instruction and involvement in their lives. Yes, life was good . . . *thank you, Father.*

Allie was relaxing in the hammock with a book when her mom called for her to round up Alan. They needed to stop by the Country

Club to pick up something before going to Nana and Papa's for dinner. How Allie loved her grandparents. They both were sweet morsels to her soul, and actually, she would not mind living with them. Things at home were great, but always so frenetic with Alan and all his boisterous friends. She loved to stay weekends at Nana's, and after church go back home for the family lunch. Her grandparents always joined them on Sunday. Sunday afternoons were all about family time. She loved her life and enjoyed her time with God and praying for Him to reveal His purpose for her life.

Anna was enjoying working through all of the details to ensure this was indeed a surprise party for her children! She felt more blessed with each passing day. God had blessed them with healthy and Godly children, blessed their finances and most of all blessed the union that she and John had. Life was too good to be true . . . *thank you, Jesus.*

"Allie, are you and Alan ready to go with me?"

"Yes, we are or at least I am. I think Alan is in his room talking on the phone to someone."

Alan bounded down the stairs in one great leap! "I'm ready for anything . . . it's my birthday! Oops, or should I say, our birthday?"

Anna pointed to the garage. "Okay, then hop in the van with me!"

"I forgot, why are we going to the Country Club first before going to Nana's?" Alan voiced with a boom.

"It is just a quick errand I need to run," Anna replied as she backed out of the driveway.

"Wonder what Nana will have prepared special for our birthday dinner tonight?" Alan chimed in again.

Allie piped up, "Maybe steak or shrimp; my favorites!"

"Whatever it is, we know she is the best cook in the world, so that part will not be a surprise! Okay, kids, we're almost there. You two can remain in the car; I'll only be a moment."

Anna went inside and made her way to the banquet hall where everything was in full swing. The music, the decorations, the friends, the banners of birthday wishes, and the fabulous aroma of seafood and grilled steaks!

"Okay everyone, let's turn off the music and lights, and I'll get the children!"

Anna quickly slipped back to the car. "Hey kids, I need more hands than I have, would you come with me for just a moment?"

Anna knew they were taking their time sensing she had drafted them into another one of her causes.

"Where are we going, Mom?"

"Patience, Alan, it is a little ways down the hall, here. Just a second while I turn on the lights."

When they entered the banquet hall, the lights, birthday music and all the well wishers really took the kids by surprise!

Alan shouted, "Whose idea was this? I just want to know!"

Allie shook her finger at her Nana and teased, "I bet I know who hatched this surprise."

Their dad spoke up and said, "Yes, this is your Nana and Papa's production. Your mom gets the credit for getting you here without your having a clue, and I'm just here for the party!"

Allie hugged her Nana and Papa and told them how much she loved them and needed them, and this was her best birthday, yet!

Alan was not nearly as expressive, but he had his ways. After finishing the main meal, he made sure he gave a piece of cake to both of his grandparents before he had any.

After enjoying their feast with family and friends, Esther and Edmond brought out their gifts for the children and presented them with smiles of adoration and such tender love.

For Alan, there was a new soccer ball, his favorite brand and a check for $1,000 to be placed toward the purchase of something he really wanted that his parents would be in favor of him purchasing.

"Nana and Papa, there are no grandparents in the whole world as great as the two of you. Thank you from the bottom of my heart!"

It was Allie's turn next. She was always a little on the shy side whenever she was the center of attention. She reached for Esther and placed a tender kiss on her cheek and then gave Edmond a sideways hug and held his hand. Oh, how these grandparents loved their grandkids. Allie was presented a beautiful leather bound Bible with her name on the front and a check for $1,000.

Allie said in a small voice, "You both know how much I love to read the Word of God, and I will always cherish this Bible. And as far as this generous check, I think I'll save this towards my expenses in Bible college. Thank you, both so very much. I love you more than you know."

John and Anna were so pleased that this had been a surprise and equally pleased that their children had an appreciation and respect for their grandparents. These kids were Esther and Edmond's motivation to stay active. These were indeed great times, wonderful memories and blessings to be counted.

Upon arriving home that evening, Anna put her arms around Allie and said, "Honey, I didn't know you were already starting to think about going to college and a Bible college at that. When did this come about?"

"Mom, it has been on my mind for a while to talk with you about a Bible college, but the timing just hasn't been right."

"Well, honey, I think it is wonderful. Do you feel that you are already being called into a ministry for the Lord?"

"I do, Mom."

"Well, Sweetheart, that is the most wonderful news and I'm so proud of this decision. We'll continue to pray that God would show you clarity and discernment in the options you'll have before you in a few years. And you know, those years will fly by before we know it."

Anna pulled her sweet daughter to her and held her close thinking how it seemed only yesterday that she was nursing and rocking this child. *Oh, God, keep Your hedge of protection around my precious daughter and guard her heart, please dear Lord.*

"Mom, I'm kind of tired. Think I'll go up and read my new Bible until I get sleepy. I love you so much. You have to know that you are the greatest mom."

Anna's heart felt that it would burst with love for her vulnerable and fragile daughter. A daughter who had always been so loving, manageable, agreeable and just easy. *Dear God, it won't be long before some guy will be wanting to take her away from her focus on her Lord. Plant your Word deep in her heart and lead her through your Holy Spirit to make decisions that would be pleasing to You for Your Kingdom purpose.*

Anna walked into the den where John and Alan were having a discussion about the wisdom of placing his $1,000 on the purchase of a horse. There was so much more to owning a horse than just the initial purchase. There were stable costs, food, riding gear, vet bills, shoes three or four times a year, and a time commitment. Anna turned around and retreated to her bedroom for some quiet time before retiring. The subject matter of a horse would simply have to be handled by John. She had no wisdom where it came to owning a horse. Actually, she nor John either one had grown up in the country. Where Alan got this love for horses was not known to her. There was simply no way to be completely peaceful about sports or horses. Both seemed to have high risks! *God, please guard my son and protect him from himself!*

Fingernail Moon

Later when John came to bed, Anna awakened to his touch. He could just look at her without even touching her, and she still had butterflies. She loved this man with a passion that only God could kindle. She would give her life for this man. He had loved her with the greatest tenderness that she could ever have imagined. He worked hard, never complained and provided all the things their family needed. He was absolutely head of household. If ever there was a Godly man, John was that man. She could always read him, and there were times still when his heart ached for his other son, Eddie. There had been times that she would hear him stirring in the middle of the night. She never intruded for she felt this was his time with God, and only God could give comfort for such a great loss as one's child.

John's mother had filled in a lot of the blanks regarding Kate and Eddie, and Anna was so thankful that John did not have that burden. It would have crushed Anna's heart to have her husband share such unspeakable things.

John pulled her close to the full length of his body and kissed her deeply.

—

As Cindy placed the finishing touches to the fresh fruit pie, which was Mayme's recipe, she found her thoughts transported to that very sad day when Mayme died. It was so unexpected, and at the same time her age did reflect she was close to that heavenly journey.

Mayme had enjoyed taking care of every detail of the wedding that fall, and the weather was so beautiful that nothing would do for Al, but to have the ceremony on Mayme's property. The setting was beside the little stream on the back part of the land. Al built an archway for Mayme to create a fresh flower covering. It was positioned close to the beautiful trees that grew on the bank of the stream by the meadow. The church folks hauled chairs in pick-up trucks, plus tables were brought from their church for the food to be placed on for the reception. The people from the church were just lovely, and Mayme was really in her element! It could not have been a more sacred and beautiful wedding.

Things may have been different had we moved in with Mayme rather than my place. There were clear signs that her heart was not as joyful. God bless Al for taking time from work each day to visit her. He said Mayme always insisted that as long as she had her sweet Jesus, she was not alone. On Sundays after church, it was so pleasant spending the rest of the afternoon at her country place. We kept those rockers hot on the front porch! Perhaps it was just God's time to call his faithful daughter home.

Dear Lord, my heart still hurts when I think how broken Al was upon finding that Mayme had apparently died during the night all alone. Those were tough times, and I know that he still hurts even though it has been several years, now. Please continue to comfort him, Lord, and build Your faith in my husband, and give him Your discernment and wisdom in all of his decisions. Thank you, Lord. And please, Father, always protect our son. I think Al worries sometimes over how some of the choices he made in his past may have a rippling effect on our future and our son. Please cover us with the blood of Jesus, Lord.

"Hey Cole, where is your dad?"

"Still in the garden. I got too tired to pick any more beans, Mom."

"It is okay, sweetie, I'm sure you were a big help to your dad. He could not have managed without you."

"Is supper ready?"

"Yes, it is. Why don't you run tell your dad to call it a day, and come eat, okay?"

"I'm going to tell him if he doesn't come now, I'm going to eat all the pie!"

"Oh, boy, that will do it!"

Cindy's thoughts raced back once again to their sweet saint, Mayme. She still found it so amazing that Mayme had bequeathed everything she owned to Al. She would be so proud to see the place now. Al had totally renovated the house. There was now an additional bedroom and bath, plus a large and spacious kitchen and a roomy den with windows across the back wall overlooking the beautiful meadow where they were married. Yes, God had been so good to them. The dress shop had been sold right before Cole was born. Dreams do come true . . . a stay at home mom taking care of her husband and son. What more could a wife and mother want?

"Hey, I'm going to quickly wash up, then we'll eat Hon, okay?"

"You better make it quick or you know who is going to eat your share of the fruit pie!"

"Hey little man, you come wash up, too."

"Oh, Dad, I washed my hands before I came to get you."

"How about that snake you were playing with?"

"Cole, you did not pick up a snake! Tell me you did not!"

Cole gave a wink to his dad and smiled at his mom. "We had you going, didn't we Mom?"

"Not fair, two against one . . . just not fair!"

Al sat down at the table. "You know how we can remedy this situation, don't you?"

"Well, we're trying, but there are simply no guarantees, are there?"

"Cindy, I believe the Lord will bless us with a little girl, and she will look just like her mother!"

"Hey Dad, you've got a great idea since I look like you!"

Al held his wife and son's hands. "Time to eat, please ask the blessing, son."

"Dear God, thank you for this day, thank you for this food and thank you for the dessert Mom fixed for me. Amen."

"Fixed for you! I guess you think you are the only one entitled to seconds?"

"Dad, you know I'll share."

"Where did this child get his sense of humor? Oh, yes, like mother, like child . . . . we already know that!"

Cindy teasingly said, "Well, since he looks so much like you, he has to act more like me. God wants a balance in this life, doesn't he?"

"Cindy, my darling, I'm confident you will always keep both Cole and me off balance!"

Cole just looked from one to the other with an amused expression on his little freckled face.

Al thought about his wife and son, and how his heavenly Father had extended His grace and mercy through his faithful servant, Mayme. How his heart ached for the conversations they had enjoyed on the front porch. Through that "sold out" woman to Jesus, his life had been totally transformed. Actually, he could not remember now when God was not the main focus in his life. When he looked at Cole, who was a small version of himself, especially with the red hair, Al knew that God was all about second chances!

He had tried to pass on those second chances to others, too. In the past couple of years, he had hired two young men to help in the hardware store. Both had potential, but just needed for someone to give them the opportunity to show their worth. Several times in the past few months he had left the store entirely to the care of Stan and Luke while he concentrated on doing maintenance jobs at the church. Pastor Jones never pressured him about things needing to be done, but when little projects were completed, he was so appreciative. Mike Jones had become Al's best friend over the years and knew things about Al that no other had knowledge of. After Mayme died Al felt compelled to tell his story to Mike. If he had not had someone to spill his guts to, he would have died in his grief. Grief over Mayme and his own life's miserable choices and sins. He did not realize that by sharing with Mike, this personal information would be the springboard for a bond such as he had never imagined, best friend and brother in Christ.

Every time Al looked at his son, he marveled at the goodness of God, his Savior and Redeemer! Cole was so bright. He had been reading the child's version of the Bible and also the sports section of the newspaper since he was about four. Cindy also read to him constantly. Cole was such a well rounded child and so much fun to be with because of his keen sense of humor. Sometimes he wondered if having another child would take away their appreciation of this precious gift from God. He truly was a wonder to watch and learn from each day. *My God, how can I ever thank you enough for all the miracles You and You alone have brought about in my life? Continue to teach me in all of Your ways, and let not my focus drift to anyone or anything else but Your boundless mercies, grace and love. Living for Jesus one day at the time, and knowing I have eternal life with You, makes every day pure joy! Protect my family and walk with us in the victories, and dear Lord, carry us in the valleys, which we know are part of this earthly plight. All praise to you, Lord.*

"Cole, it is your bedtime. Get your bath and we'll do our reading, okay?"

"Okay, Mom. I know it is your way or no way, even though I really don't like baths!"

"Go, child. Cleanliness is next to holiness, you know that."

"I know, Mom, but God sure loves to bless those vegetables in the garden, and they stay dirty all the time."

"I want to know where all this comes from? You never cease to have clever answers, do you?"

"Mom, you're the best and I love to see you laugh!"

"Then you better go now or I'll lose my clown smile! See you in about fifteen."

"Here, let me help you with the dishes, Hon."

"No, go kick back and relax, I'll have these done before our little comedian finishes his bath!"

Clay proudly walked across the stage of the auditorium and accepted his High School Diploma. Dixie thought as she watched him how much more mature he looked since a little over a year ago when they had been together for his last rodeo performance. Ms. Belle had been so upset about the newspaper article that Clay lost interest in competing after that. Fortunately, the last competition accomplished his goal for college funds.

She was so proud of him. Not only did he graduate a year early, but received special honors for high marks in school. His parents had to be proud! Her folks were hosting a dinner at the church tonight in honor of Clay. She could hardly wait to spend some time with him.

This past year away from home had definitely established the fact she wasn't as independent as she had claimed. Her stomach had churned for at least the first six weeks trying to adjust and trying not to admit how homesick she had been. As pledged to one another, she and Clay wrote letters faithfully, but she never let on in her letters how much she missed home. She had changed her mind at the last minute and accepted a scholarship to Moody rather than Brown. God was calling her first to His ministry with a secondary focus on journalism. Her first year at Moody Bible Institute was pretty basic regarding academics, which was good since everything else was a culture shock! Chicago was worlds apart from a country place like Calveston. She was confident journalism was the right major for her, and so thankful the campus environment was structured for Christians. She had her fingers crossed that Clay would join her at Moody for his undergraduate and graduate studies in the ministry. He had scholarship offers from three schools, and if he had accepted, she was not aware. This was God's department, so she did not want to ask. She knew he would share when the time was right. That was just Clay. He approached life without haste, except when he was running the barrels!

Clay strolled over to where she was standing outside the auditorium chatting with a small group from the church. "Don't you think we both deserve a summer vacation from the studies?"

"Indeed, I do!"

"Hey, would you like to ride with me to the house? It will give you a chance to enjoy our little Laura, and perhaps we'll have time for a ride before dinner. Dad purchased a new horse, and he is a charmer. You can ride him and I'll ride Boy, okay?"

"Let's do it!"

"I'm in Dad's truck. I think the last time we rode together was on our trip to Witchita for the nationals!"

"It has been over a year, but you know, Clay, the time has not flown to me. This past year was the slowest year of my life."

"You would never admit it, but I could read between the lines in your letters . . . you were homesick, big time, weren't you?"

"Time to confess. Yes, but God comforted me and gave me His strength when I wanted to quit and come home. We know it is about perseverance, don't we?"

"Well, I admit that I missed you so much, I even cried some nights."

"Oh, Clay, I'm sorry it was tough on you, too. Hope you are not still having those nightmares!"

"Perhaps we need to talk about that subject later. I could use someone to bounce things off of. You have always been a good listener, Dixie, and you never tell secrets, either!"

"Oh, yes, I can sure keep a secret! I'll put it this way, your secrets have always been safe with me. It is wonderful to have someone you can always share matters of the heart with. What do people do when they have no one they can confide in?"

"Probably just bottle it up inside until everything shipwrecks!"

"Here we are! Why don't you visit with Mom and Laura while I change clothes and get the horses saddled up. Borrow some riding clothes from Mom and come down to the stables whenever you want."

Belle opened the back door. "Dixie! Hey beautiful woman. My, how you've grown this past year!"

"Have I really?"

"That was not the correct terminology, was it? What I meant is that you've matured this last year. You are just glowing. Having a hard time turning down all those dates?"

"Right. Oh, here is the beautiful one! Laura, come see me. She looks just like you, Ms. Belle, except for that pouty mouth she got from her dad."

"She just started walking, so she is not too sure footed, so to speak!"

"Has she been horseback riding, yet?"

"What do you think?"

"I would say she has ridden with her dad and Clay."

"Correct. And I can tell you I was on the side lines kneeling and praying!"

"She has plenty of time for riding when she's older. Right now we need to play, love and hug, right?"

"We do plenty of that! This child has all three of us wrapped around her little finger."

"How does it feel having another baby? Like starting all over? I suppose it is really like having two families with Clay being seventeen and going off to college in a couple of months."

"I mostly live in the moment and try not to give much thought about Clay leaving for college."

"Oh, Ms. Belle, I didn't mean to say something that would cause you to be sad."

"Laura is a precious child and I love her so much, but there is no one quite like Clay."

"I agree. Clay is one of the most wonderful people I've ever known. We've been best friends most of our lives, and after meeting so many different people this past year at college, I realized more than ever how special Clay really is. He is a rare gem, isn't he?"

"Yes, and one who holds my heart strings ever so tightly. I cannot protect him forever, and it is not my job, anyway. I will have to trust God in all things when he departs for school. It will not be easy."

"Ms. Belle, I know Clay is a little younger than the average student for his freshman year, but he has an unwavering faith in God and a resolve to face whatever life throws at him."

"I know that is what you see, but there is a very vulnerable and fragile side to him, and sometimes it is hard for me to completely give him to God."

"Perhaps Clay will join me at Moody, and I can keep an eye on him!"

"Well, I'll let him share with you what his decision is regarding school. Don't want to steal his thunder!"

After Dixie changed into Belle's riding clothes she ran down to the stables to join Clay.

"Hope you and Mom had a nice visit. Isn't Laura a cutie?"

Oh, yes, she is beautiful and so chubby and lovable!"

"Come take a look at Prince."

"Wow, he is magnificent! Is he gentle enough for me to ride?"

"If I did not trust him, I would never suggest that you ride him, but of course, you know that!"

"I do. Why don't you give me a leg up, here. He is a tall guy, isn't he?"

"Dixie, he is an American Saddle horse with the smoothest ride you'll ever experience. I love riding him, just pure pleasure."

"You better watch it. Boy may get his feelings hurt!"

"Boy will always be my favorite horse of all times. We've been through too much together for me to ever forsake him."

"How about when you go away to school?"

"I'll be back and Boy and I will catch up then."

Boy and Prince settled into a nice pace. Boy with his slow canter and Prince with his pleasure gait. The two rode to the back of the property where rye grass was still standing, climbed down, and gave the horses their reins to nibble grass. Clay and Dixie sat down at the base of their favorite tree, where each had carved their initials, and the two relaxed hand in hand.

"Clay, it is so wonderful to just be myself. For the entire last year, I suppose I have not let down my guard. It is not that the people at school were unfriendly or did not extend themselves, but it just takes me a while to get comfortable with anyone. I've known you all my life, so it is easy to relax because I know that you only want what is best for me."

"Well, on this note, I've decided to attend Moody and come be with you, Dixie!"

"Oh, Clay, that is the most fabulous news!"

She threw her arms around his neck and he enclosed her and held her until she released him. He cupped her face in his hands, and lightly and tenderly kissed her full on the mouth. Every fiber of Dixie's body was flooded with joy and excitement. She had imagined this first kiss for well over a year, and the reality was sheer ecstasy!

"Dixie, I've wanted to kiss you for so long. I hope you are okay about my taking such liberties without first asking permission."

"Clay, the truth of the matter is I've wanted you to kiss me ever since we went to the rodeo event together last year, but really did not know if you felt the same way."

"I've missed you being here in the community so much. This place has not had the same appeal since you left. To tell you the truth, I thought my heart would break, Dixie."

"Don't tell me, Clay Samuels, that the girls are not knocking your door down."

"I've never noticed."

"True, you wouldn't!"

"I've had all kinds of jealous thoughts about your being on dates with many guys at Moody!"

"Not even one!"

"Dixie, we are quite the pair."

"Oh, Clay, I'm so glad to be in your space. Let's be done with this college talk, and just enjoy our summer together as we always have!"

"It is a deal!"

2006

Allie sat quietly on the wooden bench under a majestic oak that was becoming as comfortable as an old shoe. This was her favorite place to ponder about all the mysterious things that God spoke to her about. She had been at Moody Bible Institute for almost an entire semester. Her marks were great and she enjoyed her professors and the upbeat atmosphere of a Christian campus. Since coming to Moody, she had been troubled by and yet drawn to a graduate student named Clay Samuels. He helped Professor Smithson with his lectures. He was a fabulous speaker and placed a wise and interesting twist on everything he expounded on. She had to admit, he mesmerized her. At first she remembered just staring at him, and he would give her a quick easy smile and nod his head. He was the most beautiful man she had ever laid her eyes on. He treated everyone the same, and as far as she could tell was not involved in a relationship. For some reason she stayed consumed by thoughts of him, and really did not know why. He had certainly never given her any indication he was interested in her. *Lord, what is it about this person that haunts me? Please give me some clarity. I really don't know him, but still feel somewhat attracted. Thank you, Lord. I know You know, and that's enough.*

As Allie was walking to her Bible History class, Clay strolled up beside her.

"Hi Allie, do you mind if I walk with you?"

She was so startled, but managed to say, "Of course, that would be nice."

"Are you enjoying all of your classes?"

"Very much."

"I think you'll find that God will seek His own out and show them His Kingdom purpose here at Moody."

"Mr. Samuels, has God revealed His perfect Will to you?"

"Please just call me Clay, and while I may not yet know His perfect Will, He continues to show me grace and mercy, and I take great comfort in His rest."

"You are so young to talk about rest."

"I don't think it matters how young our years are, trouble, questions, doubts and hurts come to all of us, and His rest is where we are comforted."

"I see."

"Would you like to continue this conversation after class at the canteen?"

Allie was so taken aback, she could hardly respond. "Why yes, I think I can do that."

"Great. I'll see you there perhaps fifteen minutes after class is over."

Later at the canteen, Allie reflected on her conversation with Clay before class. He was so easy to be around, and conversed with her as though they had been acquainted for years. There was something familiar about him, and yet something strangely elusive. *Lord, guide me every step of the way. You alone know who I am going to be equally yoked with for life. I have never been remotely interested in dating, but I find myself drawn to Clay for some reason.*

Clay entered the canteen and spotted Allie right away.

"Thanks for meeting me, Allie."

"Well, I have to admit, I was somewhat reluctant, but you are so easy to talk with and too your request took me by surprise, so here we are!"

"Have you ordered anything, yet?"

"I'm really not hungry, but I would like a Dr. Pepper, my favorite drink!"

"Mine, too, I'll go get a couple. Be right back."

"Hey Allie, would you like to sit outside? It is such a beautiful day and if we sit in the sun, we'll be warm enough."

"Oh, yes, that sounds heavenly."

"Have you got plans for the Christmas holidays yet?"

"I do, I'm going home to visit my parents and twin brother."

"Wow, you have a twin! Now, that's got to be interesting."

"Actually, we are exact opposites and don't really look that much alike either, so I'm not sure why I ever mention the fact that we're twins."

"Are you close?"

"We've always communicated well, but since he is an extrovert and I'm the introvert, we do not have much common ground."

"What is your brother's name, Allie?"

"His name is Alan, and he is all about sports and horses!"

"So, I don't suppose you ride horses?"

"I've tried, but I don't think horses are any more comfortable with me than I am with them!"

"Oh, I have an American Saddle horse I bet you would fall in love with. His Name is Prince and he is as gentle as a lamb."

"So you like to ride then?"

"As a matter of fact, I love to ride. I feel blessed to have grown up on a ranch. I would not be going to school at Moody today, if I had not competed in rodeo events and saved my winnings to pay for my education."

"Oh my goodness, you are the child rodeo star who was labeled the "Ghost Rider," aren't you?"

"Your brother really is into horses, isn't he?"

"I cannot believe I'm sitting here talking with you! You are my brother's idol!"

"Well, that was a while back. I only ride for pleasure now, and since I'm so far from home, it is basically only the summers."

"I can hardly wait to talk with Alan. He will not believe me! This is just uncanny. Clay, I would really like to hear more about your life. Has the Lord called you into a specific ministry for Him?"

"Allie, I'm not sure about the specifics, but I do know that God has called me to serve Him, and for right now that's good enough."

"How about you?"

"I feel exactly the same way."

"Next weekend there is going to be a retreat on the river, and I have been asked to speak. Would you be interested in attending?"

"How far is it?"

"Only about twenty miles from here."

"Of course, but I do not have transportation. I'm sure you remember freshmen cannot have a vehicle!"

"You can ride with us, if you like. There will be many speakers, so we will probably only be involved in a day's worth of messages and music."

"Clay, I would love to accept your invitation."

"Thanks, Allie, I'm pleased."

―

Dixie's schedule was so busy. She helped with all the administrative issues at her dad's church, plus wrote articles for several newspapers for the religious section of their papers. She started off writing in their local newspaper, and had continued to get requests from concerns located in other states. She always felt her sense of humor opened more doors than her education. She loved being a journalist. She enjoyed her imagination and when coupled with her laptop, it was always a new journey and pleasant surprises. She loved writing!

Lately, Dixie had not had time to think much about missing Clay. Their three years at Moody together was sheer ecstasy, and she loved him more than she could ever express. He was her heartbeat. And now since they had so many miles between them, it was good that she kept extra busy or else she would miss her own heart. On occasion they would talk on the phone, but long distance calls were few and far between. She loved hearing his voice, and his strong suit was speaking. Hers was writing. His letters seemed to be getting further apart lately. She really wanted to talk with him, and had intended to call over the weekend when rates were down, but by the time church activities were over Sunday night, it was too late on Clay's clock for her to call. Maybe she should go ahead and call this evening. Yes, great idea.

As Dixie approached the Samuels' driveway, her thoughts went back to how things used to be when both she and Clay were together all the time. It seemed only yesterday that they were playing with Barney and riding horses together. How had the years gotten by so quickly?

Belle greeted Dixie with a big hug, and then Laura came up and wrapped herself around Dixie's legs.

"Hi Belle and sweet Laura! What are you guys up to?"

"We've been wondering when you were going to come by. You really stay busy, don't you?"

"Actually, too busy."

"Come in, beautiful Dixie and enjoy some cake and coffee with me."

"Sounds wonderful. Hey Laura! You are growing into such a beautiful young lady. Are you enjoying kindergarten?"

"I love my school, and I have a boyfriend. His name is Jacob."

"My, my we are just full of news this afternoon, aren't we? Come here and sit on my lap while your mom and I enjoy a nice visit. Who taught you to be such a polite and well mannered little girl?"

Laura formed her words so precisely, "My big brother and my mother, that's who."

Dixie immediately jumped on the subject of Clay. "When do you think that big brother will be visiting us? Maybe Christmas?"

Belle shook her head and Dixie's heart sank.

"Dixie, I'm afraid he is going to stay in Chicago during the holidays. We really don't have the money right now for his travel, and the little extra that he makes helping one of the professors doesn't add up to nearly enough."

"I'm sorry to hear that, Belle. I sure do miss him, and I know your heart grieves because he has been away for the last four and a half years."

"I try not to think about it because I know he is a grown man with choices of his own, and to be honest with you, he may never come back here to live. My boy child is making his own destiny now."

"Belle, I know he is a man, but if you'll think back, you once told me that he seemed so vulnerable to you. Do you still feel that way?"

"I guess not. You know, Dixie, you were with him for three years at Moody. Did you ever see that fragile part of Clay?"

"Maybe."

"And why? What are your thoughts?"

"I'm not at liberty to share much, but I will say that there is a part of Clay that is troubled. I even think there could be something that he subconsciously blocks."

Belle felt herself go limp and hot. She wanted to throw up or faint or just die. She had often wondered if the truth would ever surface, and lately, she had been haunted by the fact that the truth of Clay's past could be revealed.

"Are you okay Belle? You look absolutely white."

"Yes, I'll be okay. I guess I miss Clay more than I care to admit."

"I'm so sorry I upset you, Belle. Guess I better get going. I have a really busy season now that the holidays are approaching."

"Okay, dear Dixie. Take good care and come back to see us soon."

"See all of you at church. Bye."

As Dixie departed, her mind was plagued by the thought that Belle could so easily be upset where Clay was concerned. Some things just never added up, especially the thick hedge of privacy that always seemed to be so prevalent during the whole time she had known Belle and Clay. What could be so bad in one's past that an individual could actually block it out? I wonder. Clay continued to have nightmares at Moody, and at one time almost revealed the content, but then declined and said he actually felt foolish talking about something so negative. He was always in search of what God wanted him to do for His Kingdom. Pure and simply, it has never been about Clay, just his Lord. *Oh, God, give him freedom in the* truth. *Protect him and keep his spiritual eyes and ears attuned to Your perfect Will. Thank you, my sweet Jesus.*

After Dixie left, Belle found herself unable to snap back to the present. Her mind took her back to the time she had followed Clay and his mother on that initial Sunday afternoon. *Lord, I've asked forgiveness hundreds of times, and yet not once have I been able to forgive myself. It is like I have not paid my debt. Dear Jesus, please keep me in the present and cover Clay with Your constant protection. Truly, he is the most innocent person I've ever known, and I love him more than anything in this world. Help us all, dear Father. Please protect my family from my past!*

—

Clay and Allie had frequented the canteen many afternoons after their first visit together, and had become best of friends. Each had shared so much about their lives with no reservations. There was absolutely a natural connection between the two!

Clay sat at his desk thinking about the last two weeks and his attraction to Allie. He knew his heart still belonged to Dixie, but Allie was like a magnet tugging at his very being. She seemed like an old spirit he had known all his life. It was by far the most intense encounter he had ever had with anyone. They had a wonderful time at the retreat together. She was so easy to be with, and he was not aware of any pretense whatsoever. She had asked him to join her family for Christmas. The thought of riding the bus to Allie's home had crossed his mind several times, now. And the fare would be next to nothing, which really fit his pocketbook. There were many reasons he wanted to accept, but there was also a sense of betrayal to Dixie if he went. He had always shared everything with her, but just thinking about sharing this made him nauseated. *Dear Lord, I ask you to go before me and help me with this decision. I just don't know, but I know You do, so I'm depending on Your guidance. Please make it very apparent to me if I should not accept Allie's invitation. I depend on You to open and shut doors. I always want to be where Your Kingdom purpose can be furthered. Thank you, my mighty King.*

—

Giving her a little squeeze, John whispered, "Hello, my sweet Anna, and how was your day?"

"It was fabulous, Darling, and yours?"

"Actually, I enjoyed every appointment of the day. Together, Dan and I saw four new clients, and all of them were referrals."

"You have built such a rewarding practice, and Dan was a Godsend."

"Yes, and we have interviewed two new law students, who were most impressive, so they may end up joining our practice after their bar exams."

"John, do we need to expand the office space for the fourth time?"

"Perhaps, and if we do, I want to add another conference room and library. You know, I cannot stop thinking about Alan being an attorney one day, and taking my place in the practice."

"Don't think he wants to discuss such right now, though."

"I know, but I can't help dreaming and hoping."

"John, I know our faithful Lord will lead both of our children in the choices that are right for each."

"Anna, you always bring peace to my soul regarding every situation."

"Darling, it is just Jesus' work through my love for you. I love you more than life itself!"

"By the way, has Allie called and talked further about the young man coming to join us this Christmas?"

"As a matter of fact, she called today. But no decision has been made on his part. I think Allie feels somewhat disappointed that he did not accept her invitation right away."

"Well, this is certainly a different twist for her. She has never been remotely interested in anyone, and now that this could be changing, she is getting firsthand experience at being on the other side. It is no telling how many guys she has disappointed."

"John, it is hard for me to believe that Allie could actually be serious about anyone. Perhaps this is just a college chum, and she probably looks up to him since he is four or five years older than she. I really wouldn't read anything of significance into this invitation."

"You're right, of course, as usual. I know Allie is one of the most level headed individuals I've ever known, so I rest my case!"

"Oh, there is one very interesting point about this young man and I'm sure Alan will be truly disappointed if he does not join us for Christmas. Do you remember the kid who broke all kinds of records in barrel racing competition who Alan has talked about over the years?"

"Of course. The Ghost Rider?"

"Yes, his name is Clay Samuels."

"It is a small world, Anna!"

"Everything is God's design and His plan. I'm actually kind of excited about the possibility of Clay Samuels coming for Christmas!"

"Pretty incredible. Think I'll at least tell Alan that his idol is in the company of his sister!"

—

Cindy sat down in her favorite rocker on the back porch with Molly already asleep in her arms. She could not bring herself to take her to the nursery and place her in the crib. Molly was a comfort to her soul, and she loved to hold her close, especially when she was asleep.

"How are my darling little women doing?"

"Oh, Al, would you bring me a light blanket for Molly before you sit down?"

"I'll be right back."

Al draped the soft yellow blanket over their little girl. "Isn't she beautiful, Cindy?"

Don't think we could be prejudiced, now, do you?"

"I've never seen a more beautiful child, and I for the life of me cannot believe she is mine!"

"Where is Cole, Al?"

"He is mixing up some more sugar water for the bees."

"You are going to make a beekeeper out of him before he is a teenager!"

"I tell you, Cindy, he is a natural. He knows just as much as I do about this business, with the exception of the financial end, and he'll be involved in that in a few short years."

"Do you miss your hardware business, Al?"

"I miss seeing the people every day, but not the business itself. Luke has really surprised me since he took over the store. I think it makes him feel that something belongs to him, and he takes so much pride in the ownership. Thanks to Mayme's inheritance, I've been able to invest in the bee business and personally finance the sale of the store to Luke. She would be so pleased to see this place and know that we made good judgment calls on growing two businesses."

"It is great to be so grounded in our community. If it were not for the folks at the church, we would not have the land for all of our bee colonies. I really believe if the business prospers this year as much as it did last year, we quite possibly will have college funds for the children and a good retirement income."

"I pray so. I still have to pinch myself at times because of the abundant blessings God has bestowed on us."

"I believe God shows us His favor because we've always placed him first. I know we do not deserve it and I am so very thankful. I thank Him every day for bringing you to Kingston."

"God made something good out of my horrible past, and there is not a day that goes by that I do not thank Him. I will forever serve Him with all my heart and try to extend a helping hand to others as Mayme did. She taught me the way to live rather than just exist. And God helped me to forgive myself."

"You know, I've never wanted to discuss your past. But you would probably not be the man you are today without the struggles and pain you've had."

"A past with so many regrets about poor choices. If only I could have lived each day for the Lord, there would not be any regrets."

"Everyone has regrets, darling. We're just a splintered people because of the fall of Adam. Every person who lives struggles with the warfare of the evil one."

"Right, you are. We do not struggle with flesh and blood, but powers and principalities. I'm so thankful for the grace and mercy of Jesus."

"We've really gotten into some heavy conversation this evening. Wonder what brought this about?"

"Just what we were talking about—regrets of the past. I believe they always haunt one to a degree."

"Only God can right the wrong. I always pray that you will live in His rest and have His peace, darling. Let's not let satan steal our joy and destroy our hope."

"Yes, my darling, thanks for reminding me to live in God's victories, because He alone is the victor."

—

"Hello."

"Clay, I'm so glad we finally connected. It is so good to hear your voice."

"Oh, my sweet Dixie, you are a sweet fragrance to the Lord and me. I really needed to hear your voice."

"Is everything okay? I know you can't come home for Christmas, and that's got to be difficult when there will be so little going on at the campus."

"That brings up something I want to discuss with you. There is a young girl who is a freshman in the class where I do some lectures for the professor, and she has asked that I join her family for Christmas since they do not live too far from Chicago."

"Clay, is she just a student and friend, or do you need to tell me more?"

"Dixie, you are my girl, and you know my life, my heart and my soul. There is no one who can take your place."

"That still doesn't answer my question, Clay."

"I can honestly tell you that there is no chemistry between Allie and me."

"I'm relieved, Clay. God would have to breathe for me if anyone came between us or anything happened to you."

"I feel the same way, Dixie."

"What is Allie's family's name, Clay?"

"I'm pretty sure it is Marshall. Allie has a twin brother, who has followed my rodeo competition through the years."

"That will give you some common ground when you visit Christmas, then."

"I haven't accepted the family's invitation, yet. I really wanted to pray for God's leading and discuss things with you, first."

"Go, Clay. Please don't stay on campus alone when you have an opportunity to be in a family gathering for Christmas. I'm encouraging you to accept this invitation."

"I'll pray about it, and I'm sure God will lead me where He wills. But, Dixie, I want to thank you for loving and trusting me as you do."

"Love and trust is what all healthy relationships are built on, and I hope ours will forever be one of love, trust and respect."

"Me, too, Dixie. Please give everyone my love. I worry about Mom sometimes. Please try to comfort her during the holidays regarding me. I don't know what it is, but she has a hard time letting go and letting God."

"I visited with your mom the other night, and you are right about her being somewhat ill at ease with regard to things concerning you. But, you know, I've always detected that. Wonder why she has always been so protective of you?"

"As of late, I've really been thinking about that very thing. Perhaps, I'm just of the age now to begin looking back on my life somewhat."

"Don't worry, Clay. Just enjoy the Christmas season as best you can, and we'll look forward to the summer. We both stay quite busy and our lives are so crammed full. It will be summer before you know it."

"I know we need to get off the phone, but Dixie, I miss talking with you so much. Sometimes, I long to empty my soul with you."

"Clay, we can write more frequently, okay? Let's commit to that. I know I've been a little slack, and I apologize."

"Not you, but me. I've been extremely remiss. Yes, we'll start paying attention. I know you need my emotional support as much as I need yours."

"Okay, I must go. I promise to check in with your mom frequently, so don't worry. Clay, I miss you more than I can say. Please take good care of yourself and try to rest easy at night."

"I love you, Dixie."

"I love you, too. So long Clay."

"Bye for now."

"Thank you Lord, I needed to connect with Dixie to get my head back on straight. She is so grounded and yes, the love of my life. Please help me to keep things in my life in the proper perspective, especially concerning Allie."

—

Allie spotted him right away. His bus had been right on schedule, and she found a parking place at the front door of the station.

"Hi Clay, welcome to our fair city!"

"Hello Allie, it is good to be here. The trip wasn't too long, and I was able to catch up on some reading and take a quick nap!"

"Well, it is probably a good thing you grabbed a quick nap and relaxed on your journey, because the activity level of our family can reach a frenetic pace quickly when everyone gets together! My mom's folks won't be joining us, but dad's will be there, and you will love them. They are the sweetest people you'll ever meet."

"I guess sweet people run in your family, right?" He said with a soft natural smile.

"Could be."

"This will be my first Christmas away from home, so it will be nice to celebrate the Lord's birthday in a family gathering. I've really looked forward to being around a warm environment for Christmas. As you know the campus was a ghost town, however, I did get all my lectures for the first several weeks of the semester prepared. I'll have more time to work on a research paper which is due the end of January."

"Clay, you are always so organized and focused. Sometimes, you remind me of my dad."

"My mom is more single-minded than I am. It is amazing how those genes can be so strong in certain traits."

"Let's see, you have a little sister around six, right?"

"Yes, and don't you know she'll have quite a Christmas this year?"

"I hope Alan will not wear you out! He has already plotted and schemed to get you to himself. He will probably bend your ear constantly about horses and sports."

"That will be fine. After all horses were a major part of my life until college, and I could use some knowledge in the sports arena, so I won't totally be in left field conversing with other guys!"

"Okay, here we are and it looks like my grandparents are already here!"

Clay lifted his suitcase and walked to the front entrance with Allie. As they entered through the front door, the wonderful smells of Christmas hugged him, and he felt quite comfortable.

"Hey everyone, I want you to come welcome our guest."

"This is my friend, Clay, and Clay these are my parents, Mr. & Ms. Marshall, and the other Mr. & Mrs. Marshall are my grandparents, and we call them Nana and Papa, then there is my brother, Alan!"

"It is a pleasure to meet all of you, and thank you so much for inviting me to join your Christmas gathering."

"Clay, we are about thirty minutes away from dinner being ready, so Alan, why don't you show Clay where to put his suitcase upstairs." Anna broke the silence.

As Clay and Alan went upstairs, everyone got busy doing their part in preparation for the meal.

Clay was seated between Allie and Alan with Anna and John at each end of the table and Esther and Edmond across from the young adults. After Clay was asked to bless the food, everyone settled right in to passing dishes and helping their plates. Anna and Esther had done a marvelous job of preparing a meal that was fit for a king!

"Clay, Allie tells me your family lives on the western border of Texas," John said.

Fingernail Moon

"Yes, sir, that is correct. My dad is a rancher and my mom is a mother and housewife, and I have an adorable little sister named Laura. We've been there in Calveston for as long as I can remember."

"So you've always been around horses and involved in competitive riding?"

"I really cannot remember when I did not ride."

Alan piped up, "Hey Dad, I know it is Christmas and all, but I would love to take Clay over to the stables to see our horses after dinner."

"Sounds like a great idea, but don't leave your sister out!"

"Oh, I'm fine with spending time with Mom and Nana. You guys go have fun!"

"Mr. & Mrs. Marshall, you certainly have a beautiful home, here."

"Thank you, Clay, my Anna is responsible for the design, and we had a good friend who was the contractor and worked beautifully with subcontractors, so the construction of this home went smoother than we could have ever anticipated."

"Allie has also told me how fond she is of her grandparents. Do you all live in close proximity to one another?"

"Actually, we do," said Esther.

"Maybe seven miles," Edmond said.

"That had to be awesome growing up close to your grandparents! From what I hear, it is extremely easy to be spoiled!"

Anna asked, "How about you, Clay?"

"My mom's folks had passed away before I was born, and my dad's parents passed away when I was too small to remember. So I've not had the honor of enjoying loving grandparents."

Esther smiled and said, "Well, Clay, it may be more of a liability than one might think since Alan and Allie have had four very watchful and protective adults in their lives rather than two."

Allie laughed and said, "Nana and Papa have never disciplined us, only loved us!"

"I suppose that is one of the reasons they are called grand!" said Clay.

"Are we going to have your famous carrot cake for dessert, Nana?" Alan asked.

"Absolutely, and it is still warm, so shall I get a slice for everyone? Clay, how about you?"

"Thank you, Ms. Marshall, a small slice. I'm not much on sweets."

Alan spoke up. "Clay, I absolutely guarantee you, if your slice is small, you'll be looking for another slice before bedtime tonight!"

Everyone laughed and agreed.

Later that night when Clay was reflecting on the day's activities, he looked out the window beside his bed and to his delight discovered a fingernail moon nestled in a sky full of stars. It took him back to the time when he was little and felt so secure sleeping with his mom and Barney. He had not thought of Barney in a long time. Even now, it was hard to think about Barney without a deep ache in his heart. Sometimes when he thought of him, he would have the strangest thoughts to dart through his mind. It always felt as though he had a few pieces to a puzzle, but could not envision the whole picture. Somehow his mind would just stifle any further thoughts down that path.

Allie had a nice family, and he felt comfortable with all of them. There were several times he remembered Nana Marshall staring at him, which come to think of it seemed a bit odd. One time, he thought he saw tears in her eyes. Well, he sure enjoyed her carrot cake, and the taste was like nothing he had ever eaten, and yet it was so wonderfully familiar in a strange kind of way. Actually, it was his first time ever to eat carrot cake. Anyway, it was satisfying to the tips of his toes! He had enjoyed his time at the stables with Alan. They had ridden for a couple of hours together, even raced from the back of the pasture to the barn. Alan had the faster horse, and boasted about his victory, which Clay found amusing. Allie was much more mature than her brother, but Alan was a great guy to have fun with, and Clay would always enjoy riding horses with him. It amazed Clay that Alan had kept all the old newspaper clips from his competition days. A couple of times Alan asked him how he got the name "Ghost Rider," but the answer never seemed to surface. *Lord, I miss my family so much. I trust they have had a wonderful Christmas day. Please help Mom's heart to be light and enjoy Dad and Laura to the fullest with no pining for me. Dear Father, help Mom to relax more and just enjoy the moment. Help her to totally drop her guard and rest in You and You alone knowing that You will be with her every step of the way in this life. Just keep her from worry, dear Lord. Please be with me tomorrow on my bus trip back to the college, and comfort me throughout the rest of the holidays since I'll be without family and my very best friend, Dixie. I ask all of these things in Your precious Name, Jesus. Amen.*

Esther was having her coffee on the patio when Edmond came out to join her. He sat down beside her, and waited for her to greet him. Usually, he would not disturb her while she was reading and having quiet time with the Lord in the mornings.

"Esther, are you okay?" Edmond inquired.

"I'm not sure."

"What do you mean, you're not sure. Are you feeling ill?"

"Edmond, what I'm about to say may sound totally bizarre to you, but hear me out, and just think about it."

"I'm listening, Sweetheart."

"Do you think Clay could be Eddie?"

"I don't follow you, Esther."

"There is something about Clay that reminds me of Eddie. And yes, I know Eddie was just a child when we last saw him, but there is something in the eyes and perhaps the smile that remind me of Eddie and John."

"We still look for Eddie in every young man, and probably always will, but I don't think from what Clay shared of his family history, there would be any connection whatsoever."

"Edmond, we do not know. Eddie could have been kidnapped, sold or adopted. Who knows what all could have happened during the course of his young childhood."

"Clay certainly seemed to be quite sure of his childhood, and he is such a confident and secure young man, who seems to have a very well adjusted life."

"I know, Edmond. I totally agree, but there is still something there that raises the question. We must trust the Lord for all things. He will bring about things in His timing."

"Absolutely, Esther. Now you relax and let the peace of Jesus ground you."

"Helloooo. Anyone at home?"

"Alan, we're on the patio. Come on in."

"Hi. Just got back from taking Clay to the bus station. Isn't he a great guy?"

"Yes, Alan, he is a fine young man. Your Nana and I were just talking about him. Pretty interesting about how you've followed him through the years when he was in barrel racing competition. What a stroke of luck for you to finally meet your idol."

Esther asked, "Do you think your sister is serious about this young fellow?"

"I have no idea. If she is it certainly did not show. And actually, Clay did not seem to be taken with Allie. I would say they are good friends, and that's it."

"Well that's good."

"Why is that good, Nana?"

"Well, I don't know. Allie is still quite young with plenty of time to pursue romance after she finishes her education."

"I can tell you, I would like to see more of him. He is a very interesting and wise individual, and so easy to be around. I think he would be a great addition to our family!"

―

"Hi Mom!"

"Clay, it is so good to hear your voice! I've missed you more than I can say, especially since this is the first time we've been separated during the Christmas season. Dixie told us you were invited to spend Christmas Day with the family of one of your students."

"That's right, and I thoroughly enjoyed myself!"

"Clay, is this someone you might be interested in?"

"Funny, that you would ask, Mom. It is a rather unique relationship that Allie and I have. I would have to say we are definitely connected in a comfortable way, but without the chemistry. Does that make sense?"

"Sounds like you two have common ground that embraces easy communication."

"Well said, Mom. That's it!"

"Clay, I've never really asked you about Dixie, and often wondered since you spent three years together at Moody."

"Mom, Dixie is so much a part of me, and has been all my life. I've been waiting on the Lord concerning our relationship. Certainly, you must know I love Dixie, but for some reason, I'm not totally confident about making any commitment at this point in my life."

"You have plenty of time. I'm sure the Lord will reveal His Will for your life."

"I have to tell you, Mom, there is something about Allie Marshall that continues to draw me to know more about her."

"Her last name is Marshall?"

"Right, and I was so taken with her whole family. They are all so grounded in the Lord and are such loving people."

Belle remembered that Dixie had told her that Clay was visiting a family in the same city where she had lived before coming to Calveston. And now, the name Marshall sent electrical shocks through Belle's entire body. Had to be a coincidence . . . . certainly, there were many "Marshalls" who would not be connected to her Clay.

"Mom, are you still there?'

"I am, Sweetheart."

"You were so quiet, just thought I had lost you, there."

"Tell me more about your new friend. Her family sounds interesting."

"Really, not a lot to tell, as I only spent a short time with them. Allie does have a twin brother, and I got to meet Mr. Marshall's parents, too. They were just lovely people. I would have to say Allie's family is grounded in their Christian walk like Dixie's folks. I felt completely at home and most welcomed."

Belle found her mind racing and her heart beating wildly. She felt compelled to ask one more question. "Clay, what is Mr. Marshall's first name and what does he do for a living?"

"That's an odd question, Mom, but Allie's Dad's name is John and he is a practicing attorney."

Belle remembered vividly the one article she read in the newspaper after she kidnapped Eddie, and John Marshall, an attorney was the mentioned father! This was the nightmare she had played over and over in her head through the years.

"Mom, are you okay?"

"Yes, son, I'm fine. Guess I better let you go. Please always remember how much I love you."

"I love you, too, Mom."

"Bye, Sweetie."

"Good-bye, Mom."

Belle ran to the bathroom and threw up. She felt as though she were going to faint. She actually wished she could just die! *Oh, My Lord, help me, please. Right my wrongs, Father. Please do not punish my family. Should the truth come out, this will kill Les, and what about my sweet Laura? Oh, Lord, what shall I do? Help me, Lord . . . .*

Belle walked back into the kitchen and sat down at the table where Les was reading.

"My word, Belle, what's the matter? You look awful."

"I just vomited, and feel wretched."

"Well, honey, let's get you to bed, and I'll bring you a cold cloth for your head."

"Les, would you call Claire, and ask if Laura can just stay the night with them, and we'll pick her up tomorrow when I feel better?"

"Of course, right away, my darling."

Belle's head was spinning with a thousand negative thoughts at one time. There was nothing she could play out in her head that would ease her pain. Not one thing! Why had she kidnapped Eddie? But if she had not, she would never have known the wonderful and tender times with Clay, and he would not be the person he is today, nor would she. Who would have protected him all these years? And yet Clay, himself, said that the Marshalls were wonderful people. Perhaps their lives were changed only because of the loss of Eddie. Sometimes, it is only in the valleys that one draws really close to the Lord. Just maybe John Marshall's life is like the account of Job's in that he is more blessed now with his new family. Just maybe, just maybe I'm all undone for nothing. There could certainly be more than one John Marshall in a big city! Yes, that's it. I've let my imagination run wild. *Jesus, Jesus, Jesus please give me Your peace.*

"Feeling better now?"

"Yes, isn't it amazing what a cold cloth will do for nausea?"

"Talked with Claire, and she is pleased that Laura will be staying the night, but concerned about you. I told her it was probably just a twenty-four hour virus. You would be fine tomorrow."

"Les, please get in bed with me. I just need to be held."

"Thought you would never ask!"

"Sometimes, I get consumed with my past mistakes and the wrong choices I made in my life and it haunts my very soul."

"Darling, you are one of the most wonderful people I've ever known. You don't have one selfish bone in your little body."

"There was a time when I was selfish, careless and foolish, though."

"Yes, and I believe the last time I checked you were still human."

"Les, please pray for me. I need the peace of Jesus."

Les pulled Belle close to him and caressed her beautiful wavy hair. She was the best thing that had ever happened to him, and he loved her with a passion. Her eyes always gave her heart away. They were so compassionate and could read your very soul. *Lord, I come to You tonight on behalf of my beautiful wife who you gave to me. I ask that you protect her and guard her heart from anything negative. Give her Your peace, Jesus, and fill her with full assurance of Your promises. I ask that You heal her mind and body, and help her to live only in the present knowing she can trust You totally with her life and the lives of her loved ones, especially Clay wherever he is and whatever he is doing. Keep Your Holy hand on our young man, and bring him safely home soon. I ask these things in the mighty Name of Jesus. Amen.*

"Oh, Les, I miss Clay so much that I believe my heart is going to break."

"We're not going to let that happen. I tell you what I believe we can swing. Why don't we fly Clay home for spring break?"

"Oh, Les, could we?"

"I've been toying with the idea of boarding some of Mr. Kennedy's mares who are expecting this summer. They really need more food than the other horses in his pasture, and he told me he would pay me $200.00 per month. There would be enough profit to cover a plane ticket for Clay."

"You know how to make your woman happy, Les."

"I would imagine it will make another woman happy, too. Our Dixie!"

"Oh, yes, you are so right. I so want Clay and Dixie to have a good life together. I don't think I've ever wanted anything more."

—

As Cindy watched Cole suit up to service the bees on their property, she felt both a sense of pride and humility. He was growing up so fast. It wasn't so much his physical growth, but his mental and spiritual maturity. She and Al could trust him with responsibilities that most people would expect only from an adult. He had become active in their church choir, too, and had begun to travel around to different churches in the area. God had given him a wonderful tenor voice, and he used it for His Glory. The church was getting invitations daily for the little quartet to travel and minister in song to young people. Between his duties with the bee colonies, church activities and school, Cole never had one idle moment. He seemed to thrive in being productive. Al had gotten more involved with the marketing aspect of their honey business. He had started traveling to some of the larger cities to talk with store owners about supplying the local customers with "Kingston's BEST" raw honey. God continued to increase their business and profits soared. Al hired two local men to help service the bees on other properties. He always gave the unfortunate a chance to make their way. One young man had served a two year prison sentence for stealing a car. Al could always see potential in all those who were down on their luck. God blessed everything Al touched. Cindy was so proud of both of her men. Molly was crawling everywhere and trying to pull up and walk. She adored her brother, and many afternoons before dinner, Cole would rock Molly and humor her during her fretful times. Dinner would have never been on time, if Cole had not taken care of Molly each evening.

There were times when Cindy felt their life was too good to be true, but then there were other times when she listened to Al lament over his previous life and how he wasted so many years that could have been lived for God. God had a way of keeping them grounded in humility. Al was never far from reliving his valleys. She wondered if that would ever change. We must never forget to give God the Glory for past victories. Only through Him will we be victors!

"Cindy, my love, are you day dreaming again?"

"Oh, it is so good to see you! How was your trip?"

"Good. We have three more grocery stores to supply. What do you think about that?"

"Wow, where all did you go?"

"Believe it or not, I went back to my birth place, St. Louis."

"Al, you didn't."

"Yes, I took the emotional plunge, and also visited my old neighborhood. Mr. Walker is still living and remembered my mom and me. We visited for a couple of hours and had a cup of tea. Kind of reminded me of my chats with Mayme."

"I'm proud of you, darling, for going back and facing some of your fears. I know you feel somewhat liberated, don't you?"

"Perhaps. There are still some things I wish I could set right and maybe one day I will, but for now, what's for dinner?"

"Let's have a small slice of fruit pie and some tea first, okay?"

"Terrific! Where are my two angels?"

"Molly is still napping and Cole is servicing the bees out back."

"Can't wait to hold them both! Being gone for four days is just a bit too much. Don't care to travel that much. Did you do okay by yourself with both children?"

"I did, but we all missed you. Here you are. I think the pie is still warm."

"Wonder if Mayme is still enjoying her fruit pies in Heaven?"

"Guess we'll have an answer to that one day, darling."

"Dad!"

"Hey, little man. How's it going?"

"Just great. All the queens are healthy right now and honey overflows. Hope you have more stores for us to fill!"

"I was just telling your mom that we have three new stores in St. Louis."

"Wow, Dad, will you take me with you sometime? I would love to visit St. Louis."

"We'll see what can be done about that. When I need to go back, perhaps your mom will let you travel with me. That is if school is out!"

"Maybe Mr. Matt and Mr. Jeff could do my bee duties while we're away."

"That's a great idea. By then, we'll know if they can handle things for us!"

"Hey, Mom, are you going to serve me up a piece of pie before dinner?"

"Just this time, but don't expect this to become a habit!"

"This is a celebration because the chief is back home!"

Al looked at Cindy. "Where does he get this stuff? It just cracks me up!"

"Hey Dad, you know you're the greatest, and we need to take every opportunity to celebrate you!"

"Talking about a fan club, you both really know how to puff up your man!"

"Cole, go fetch your little sister. I need a group hug."

—

Allie and Clay were sitting under her favorite oak tree on campus. They had enjoyed a light dinner at the grill, and decided to wrap warmly, sit outside in Allie's favorite place and catch up on each other's lives. Things had been extra busy for Clay with his research paper, and for some reason neither had mentioned spending time together on the weekends. Clay had stepped back somewhat from the relationship after their Christmas celebration with Allie's family. He really could not say why because her family was wonderful, warm and loving and so was Allie. For some reason though, God placed his spirit in check regarding his relationship with Allie.

"Clay, I've really missed our conversations. I've actually wondered if something at our Christmas gathering upset you, since you've been a little distant."

"Absolutely not. Your family is great and I could not have had a better time with all of you!"

"I'm relieved to hear that."

"I've turned in my research paper, and once again prepared my lectures for the next month, until I get back from spring break."

"Where are you going, if you don't mind my asking?"

"Mom called right after Christmas, and she and Dad are sending me a ticket to fly home."

"Clay, that is wonderful!"

"I was so very surprised. My parents have always been so frugal with their money, and it will only be a short time before our summer break, so going home in March was really a surprise to me!"

"I'm happy for you, Clay."

"Thanks, Allie. Oh, look, there is a fingernail moon! Can you see it?"

"Wow, my dad has always called a crescent moon a fingernail moon, too!"

"I remember my mom using this term when I was very young!"

"Well, we have some parallels, don't we?"

"I suppose we do, Allie. You know, sometimes when we are talking about your family, I get the feeling that somehow we're connected. Have you ever felt that way?"

"Clay, I've never mentioned this, but now that you brought it up. I feel that we could actually be kin to one another in some way. We've never talked about family names or relatives that much, but I'm certain the Holy Spirit has brought to my attention that you are connected to my life. This may sound odd, too, but you actually remind me of my dad at times!"

"Do I look his age, maybe?"

"Oh, don't be silly! You know what I mean."

"With all the miles between our families, that would have to be fairly remote, but stranger things have happened, right?"

"Our God has His perfect design interwoven in our lives, and I do believe we are all connected in some way."

"Such a wise young woman you are, Allie."

"Clay, I feel so very comfortable with you. Let's keep in touch more than we have been these last two months, okay?"

"It is a deal. I enjoy your company, as well, Allie."

"Clay, has God revealed any specifics to you regarding a ministry for Him?"

"No, Allie, and at times I do concern myself with regard to the lack of direction. But I also know that He holds my future, and I'm to trust totally and remain content where I am."

"That's the only way we can rest in Him."

"Just how did you become so wise at such a young age, Allie?"

—

Dixie was beside herself with excitement! It had been so long since she had been with Clay that she really did not know what to think regarding where their relationship stood at this point. During telephone conversations, he had always seemed to be the same steady and gentle Clay, and yet she did not sense that their relationship was going forward. Clay had no specific direction for a career, and rarely spoke of the future. As time moved forward he seemed to have less direction about anything in his future. Most of the time she did not think upon their relationship, as she was so busy with her newspaper articles and helping in an administrative capacity in her dad's church. Her God given talents and education had equipped her to make a living and also fulfill her potential. She was quite satisfied with her professional life, and her personal life to a degree, but she really felt that it was time to go forward with a relationship with Clay or turn loose of it. She had many suitors, but had never even remotely been interested in dating anyone but Clay. Perhaps his visit home this week would give them an opportunity to know if they had a future together.

Dixie had stopped to see Belle last week, and inquire about the exact time Clay would be arriving, and she noticed that Belle seemed preoccupied and distracted. Actually, Belle had not been herself in quite a while. It was as though something was tormenting her, and she was literally struggling. Dixie was cautious about her conversation with Belle, because she never knew when something she said would upset her. Belle seemed so fragile these days. Maybe things would get back to normal when Clay came home. She certainly hoped so.

Clay would be arriving late afternoon, but Dixie did not plan to see him until he initiated a visit. He needed some time with just his family, especially his mom. She knew her mom and dad had planned dinner at their place for everyone a couple of nights later, so that gave her something to anticipate. She would be busy helping her mom with all of the preparation, and there were always things she could do to help her dad out at the church. *Dear Lord, you know what is best for all of us, and I ask that Your Will be done. All things are in Your caring hands, and I'm confident You will do what is right for each of us.*

―

Clay positioned himself at the table in the exact spot he had had for years. They all held hands, and he said the blessing. As he prayed, his thoughts were more on his mother than anything else. She looked much older and thinner. He perceived that there was something serious going on with her, and hoped they would have a chance to speak alone with one another soon. He planned to question her about his past, too. He continued to have horrible nightmares, and perhaps having a candid talk with his mom would give him some insight into all of this.

Laura spoke up. "I'm so glad to have my big brother home again. Are you going to stay this time, or do you have to go away again?"

"My sweet Laura, I'm here for only a week, but in two short months, I'll come visit longer. Who knows, I may take a break and stay here for the first summer semester!"

"That would make our mom so happy, Clay!"

"Hey, that would make your dad pretty happy, too," Les said with a broad smile.

Clay changed the subject. "Mom, you have not lost your touch in the kitchen. This meal is heavenly."

"Thanks, son, but you must remember what you are comparing it to. Cafeteria food is not the greatest in the world!"

"You are right about cafeteria food, but I've always loved your cooking, and you seem to be in your glory in the kitchen."

"It wasn't always this way, but having a family can change so many things. Yes, I would have to say, I'm my happiest in the kitchen when I know my family will be gathered around our table enjoying food and fellowship! Clay it is so good to have you home where you belong."

"Oh, I can see you all are conspiring to keep me here, right? I would not want to get your hopes up, but actually, I've not had any direction regarding what I'll be doing after graduation in December. Dad, I have had some thoughts about helping you, and being a rancher, myself."

"Son, how about your commitment to the ministry?"

"I have not been called by God into a specific ministry, yet. I know that I'm comfortable in the pulpit, but not really led to be a pastor, so while I'm waiting for God to open the right door, I would like to plan to come back here, so we could build your business together. What do you think, Dad?"

"I'm speechless. This is the best news you could have possibly shared with us."

Belle was softly crying. "Clay, you've made me the happiest mother in the world!"

"Well, that's always a good thing." Clay rose from his chair and gathered his mom into his arms. Yes, he knew this was a good plan. *Thank you, Lord, for my precious family . . . what would I do without them?*

"Mom, I wonder if you feel up to our discussing some things tonight? Actually, some things regarding my past that I don't seem to remember."

Belle knew this was the bomb! "Of course, son. It is pleasant enough on the back porch and we have quilts if it gets chilly. Les, would you and Laura mind cleaning the kitchen this evening?"

"Sounds good to me! Afterwards, I'm going to get Laura to play that new board game with me. We'll learn it, and then teach it to you guys later. Does that sound like a plan?"

"Yes, Les. You're an angel. You and Laura, both."

Clay gently guided his mom to the back porch and settled her in her favorite chair with a soft quilt. He took the rocker across from her, and grabbed a quilt for himself. All of a sudden, there was a definite chill in the air. He looked up into the night sky filled with tens of thousands of bright stars, and his breath was taken away by a beautiful fingernail moon!

Belle reached across and gently cupped Clay's hand in hers. "Clay, it is time that I shared some facts with you about your past. I knew that this day would come, but hoped that it would not. You and I both know the truth sets us free, and it is time that you knew the truth even though it is going to be extremely difficult to hear. I've prayed and prayed about this for years, and I know there will be some grave consequences, however, I'm certain God will get us all through this valley and use it for His glory. I have to believe He will show His tender mercies or I simply could not get through this."

"Mom, what is all this seriousness about? I've never heard you even remotely talk like this."

"Son, while I've got the courage, hear me out. This will not be easy for me or for you either, but you have to know the truth. I pray you receive this without judging me too harshly."

"Mom, I have never judged anyone, and certainly not my mother!"

"Well, here we go, my precious young man, and the person I love most and would die for in a heartbeat. Clay, I've always been amazed at how you live in the present. You've never questioned past events or as far as I know been one to reflect on the past. You have such a wonderful acceptance of the moment in which we live. That in itself has made it remarkably easy to sweep the haunting events of our past under the rug, so to speak. Son, if it is possible for you, I would like for you to listen to my story from beginning to end before you raise questions, okay?"

"Sure, Mom. It's a deal."

"Years ago when you were a little toddler, I worked in a law firm where we would help people adopt very young children. Most of these children came from families who had abused them and were unfit parents. The welfare system would take over the care of such children, and eventually find couples who were good candidates to take care of them. And just maybe the very thing I was involved in every day somehow shaped me in the way I perceived things and my very actions."

"Mom, you are not making sense, here."

"Just here me out, Clay. This is so difficult for me."

"Okay, promise. I'll listen until you are finished."

"This is the hard part, so pray for me, please, Clay. One Sunday afternoon, a long, long time ago, when I lived in St. Louis, I visited a park on the north side of town, and witnessed what I thought was abuse to a beautiful little boy. It was so plain to see that his mother was caught up in her own problems, and her little boy was ignored and seemed to be thrown away. Of course, this bothered me and hurt my heart. When the mother and child left the park, I decided to follow them. I really thought I would feel better about things to see where they lived. Anyway, I followed them to their house, and took note of the address. The next day, I felt compelled to drive through the neighborhood again. I witnessed this little boy on his tricycle out alone quite a ways from his house, and this in itself really disturbed me. I stopped and started a conversation with the little guy. He was in such a stew trying to find his little dog, so he was not going to be detained, and pedaled faster and farther away from his home. This absolutely broke my heart that apparently his mother did not care that this precious child of hers was in danger being so far from the house."

"I pondered all these things that night when I went home. I even dreamed or had a vision of what was to come in this little one's life. I was absolutely consumed by what could happen to this innocent little child. The next morning I got in my car and drove back to the boy's neighborhood. When I started down the street where he lived, I witnessed an older model car driving rather fast. I just knew something was wrong, so I drove up in the driveway, and thought I could investigate whether or not the little lost dog had been found. The door to the kitchen through the carport entrance was open, and I could see the little boy standing next to his mother, who was on the floor in a pool of blood. After entering and looking closely, I knew she was dead. Everything in me wanted to protect this precious little boy, who called himself Eddie. I bent down and hugged him, and asked him where his little dog was. He bounded out toward the back yard, called his dog, and I scooped them both up, placing them in my car and driving off. I soon stopped at a payphone and called the police to tell them the address of the crime. I could not even imagine what the life of this little boy had been like, so I only had thoughts of how to protect him, love him and give him a life that would give him a chance."

As Belle took a survey of the expression of Clay, she wondered if she detected relief. He did not seem unsettled in the least. She decided to pose the question, "How are you doing with all of this? Are you okay?"

"I'm okay, Mom. Actually, this clears up the reason I've had nightmares for so long, and these nightmares are always the same. I'm with someone who is lying in a pool of blood, and I'm immobilized from the horror of things! The little dog was Barney, and I'm the little boy, right?"

"There is much more to this story, Clay."

"I'm sure there is, Mom, but you know what? I've heard plenty for the moment. I really want to digest what you've shared, and perhaps we can continue later."

"Clay, I hope you are not skirting around having more knowledge about your past."

"Oh, no, Mom, I want to know, but I don't want to forfeit present moment blessings with all of you and a special girl named Dixie! God will bring about the right opportunities for us to discuss the rest of what you need to share with me. We must trust His timing."

"Clay, you are without a doubt the kindest soul I've ever known. The easiest person to love, adore and cherish. God has blessed me abundantly, and no matter how our lives shake out, I could not have had a better life because of what you have given and taught me. You, son, have so much Godly wisdom. I am humbled to know you."

"Mom, you have given me the best life anyone could have ever dreamed or imagined having, and for that I'm deeply indebted."

"Well, okay, son, we shall continue when God leads. Guess you are excited about seeing Dixie, right?"

"Yes, I really want to see her tonight. That is if you don't mind my spending time with her rather than staying here with family."

"Go, with my blessings."

—

Clay gave Dixie a call and asked if she would mind driving over and meeting him in the stables for a chat. He could not wait to see her. In view of this new information from his mom, he actually felt relieved. Finally, he understood why he had the same nightmare over and over again.

He turned a few lights on, and checked on Prince and Boy. They were genuinely glad to see him. He pulled some blankets out of the tack room and spread them on the hay thinking he would like to sleep in the stables tonight. It would be nice to find a spot so he could enjoy the spring sky with all of its twinkling lights and reminders of how small and insignificant he was in comparison to the vast universe.

He could see the beam of a flashlight getting closer, and could hardly contain his excitement over Dixie!

"Clay, where are you? The lights are so dim I can't see where to walk."

She squealed as he grabbed her and swung her round and round. "Wow, you've gotten stronger since the last time we were together!"

Clay held her close, and then lifted her chin and kissed her with passion that he did not know he possessed. He wanted this moment to last forever. His whole being felt like it was being swept away in total abandonment. He knew Dixie was his soul mate. She was without a doubt the woman he would want by his side for the rest of his life.

"Clay, you are taking my breath away!"

"Well, you take mine away, too, beautiful woman. I had forgotten anyone could be so beautiful. Oh, Dixie, you are the love of my life. Do you know that?"

"I've been wondering."

"Wonder no more, my love."

"Clay, I've never seen you like this."

"God's timing, I suppose. Hey, I found a few warm blankets and spread them out in some soft hay. We can lie down and gaze at the stars and talk all night!"

"Clay, you seem so excited. Have you got something on your mind?"

"A lot, actually. My mom and I had a talk this evening, and what she shared cleared up some stuff for me. You know how I've had those horrible nightmares for years?"

"Well, yes, I remember that you had them, but you never could bring yourself to share the details."

"You are going to find this both interesting and enlightening."

All of the things his mom told him, he shared with Dixie. He watched every move she made and every perplexed expression.

"Now, please, Dixie, tell me how you feel about all of this?"

"Clay, I'm really not surprised."

"You are kidding, of course."

"No, I'm not. Your mom is one of the most private people I've ever known, and she has always been overly protective of you."

"You have a point there."

"You know, Clay, I believe there are many more things you have blocked because you were traumatized by that experience of seeing your biological mother dead. Do you even vaguely remember the incident?"

"I definitely do not, but it is certainly the way my nightmares play out."

"Since you have knowledge of what actually happened now, more details of your past could start surfacing."

"I could not wait to tell you about this and get your 'take' on things. Anyway, I believe Mom needed a break from sharing more tonight. I have never seen her so white and frail."

"I've noticed how strained your mom has seemed for quite some time now. I've really been concerned because she is always preoccupied and a little sad."

"She is going to be better, now, I just know it. Can you imagine the weight she has carried for so many years? And since I have blocked so much, I've never wanted to question the things that happened when I was very young. You and Mom both have mentioned on numerous occasions how I live only in the moment, never questioning the past or speculating on the future. Now, we know why, don't we?"

"Absolutely. Too much pain to delve into the past, and too much uncertainty to talk about the future."

"We've always said that the truth sets us free, and now I'm realizing just how true that statement is."

"Clay, with this new information, you may find yourself wanting to know about your biological parents."

"Sure don't feel inclined to know at this point. Matter of fact, I'm just thankful my mom found me and provided me with a second chance in life. Dixie, I could not have had a better life! And from the little that Mom has shared, I don't think my biological parents were fit to even have a child. I'm so thankful God worked things out the way He did, and loved me enough to give me a new life!"

"Oh, Clay, you are such an inspiration to everyone who knows you."

"Just how much influence do I have over you, beautiful woman?"

"What kind of question is that, now?"

"I know I'm not in a position to ask this of you right now, but for some reason, I need something solid in my future. I need to dream of good things, and you are who I dream to be with, Dixie. Will you be my wife?"

Dixie had never been more shocked. Maybe it was just the timing of everything or lack of timing since Clay had no real career direction. She was at a loss for words.

"Has my heart led me to believe something that yours does not feel?"

"Oh, no, Clay, I love you with all my heart, but the timing of your proposal caught me by surprise!"

"Just how long does this romantic guy have to wait for an answer?"

"Clay, the answer is yes. Yes, I want to be your wife more than anything, and I suppose we'll work out all the details regarding our careers as the Lord leads, right?"

"Absolutely, He is in the driver's seat! I suppose I need to share my thoughts regarding my intent after I finish my education?"

"Yes, that would be nice."

"I'm coming back here to help Dad. I know we could expand the cattle business and even improve our quarter horse business. I mentioned this to Mom and Dad tonight, and both were so relieved and happy about this decision. And there is more, if the Lord leads. I would like to be a lay preacher or even a part-time evangelist. There would be plenty of churches relatively close where I could step in when the pastors needed some time off. Anyway, those are my thoughts right now, and I know God will go before us as we desire to be in His perfect Will."

"Oh, Clay, that sounds wonderful. I have to admit I'm rather attached to this community and Dad's church. Actually, you could be a big help in our church, too. It has grown so much during the last couple of years. For quite some time now, I've wondered if we would have a life together should you end up settling down hundreds of miles from here."

"Hey, girl, we are officially engaged, and I'm a poor man with no money to purchase an engagement ring for my bride. Imagine that!"

"Well, all I have to say is you better start saving up, mister!"

He grabbed her and held her so tightly, she could feel her pulse beating in her temples. The night had such a crisp bite to it, and the stars were so bright, that no light was needed from the moon. They wrapped up in each other's arms and lay quietly looking up at the vast night sky. How good it felt to know they belonged to one another. They had been together most all of their lives, and this commitment was just another piece to the divine puzzle God was helping them put together.

"Clay, it is getting late, so I really need to get back home. Would you like to join us for breakfast in the morning?"

"Absolutely, I've got to ask your dad for your hand. We want to be respectful and ask for his blessings, right?"

"Yes, by all means."

"I'll walk you to your car, and then I'm coming back here and sleeping under the stars tonight!"

"It won't be long before we can do that together, and I can hardly wait!"

He pulled her close and felt the whole length of her body pressed against his. How he longed for her to be his wife now.

―

Al had been sitting and listening for hours since 1:00 that afternoon. This meeting had brought all the investors, marketing folks and managers together. "Kingston's BEST" honey had swept the country with sales that needed all the proper people in place to run such a business. A few months back a large corporation had contacted Al about selling his bee business. After much discussion, Al had offered to sell 49% for two million, and give rights to the corporation to run the business, and market the product world-wide. He knew that the business could make millions with the right people in charge, and since he had 51%, he could be as involved as he wanted to be. Presently, he received 5% of the profits without lifting a finger. This contract could be renewed or renegotiated in two years. His bee business had outgrown him all too quickly, and he was sure God had devised the perfect plan for the professionals to take over and enhance operations and marketing strategies to enable the business to thrive. Richard James had been hired on as CEO several months ago, and from that time everything fell into place so that profits soared beyond everyone's expectations. Richard was a personable guy with a genuine heart and an exceptional mind for business. Al really liked him, and was made to feel a part of every fiber of the business.

It was just after 5:00 and the meeting was coming to a close. Al was getting excited about getting back to his hotel room, calling Cindy and packing up to go home the next morning.

Ms. Marks, Richard's administrative assistant, knocked on the conference room door rather loudly, and announced, "Mr. Statham, you have an emergency call on line two, could you come quickly?"

Al quickly rose from his seat and followed Ms. Marks to a private office next to the conference room.

"Mr. Statham, I believe this may be your pastor on the line."

"Thanks, Ms. Marks, would you please shut the door behind you?"

"Mike, is that you?"

"Yes, Al. Al, I have some bad news, and I'd rather do anything than tell you over the phone, but it is necessary for you to come home quickly."

"Is it my wife or is something wrong with Cole?"

"Oh, Al, Cindy and Molly were killed instantly in a horrible car accident about an hour ago."

Al's heart felt as though it had been ripped out of his chest. *How can I take this, dear Lord? Take it for me, Lord. Carry me . . . YOU ARE ABLE . . . .*

"Al, are you still with me?"

Al could hardly get his lips to move. "How about Cole?"

"Cole is fine. He was at school, and is now at our house with Karen and our children. Al, listen to me. I'll come get you. I'm not sure it is advisable that you drive back by yourself."

"No, that won't be necessary. I'm on my way, now. Hold tight to Cole, and begin making any arrangements you think are necessary in my absence."

Mike and Karen treated Cole like he was their own. Cole had grown up with their children, and the loss of Cindy and Molly was like losing family. Their hearts ached for Cole and Al. When Karen picked Cole up at school, he of course, wondered if anything was wrong. He was such a perceptive child. She had told him that his mom and sister had been in an accident, and Pastor Mike was on his way home with the details. When they pulled up in the drive way, Mike's car was already there.

Mike placed his arm around Cole and asked him to sit beside him on the couch while Karen busied herself with their children in the kitchen. Cole listened calmly to every detail Mike shared. After Mike had finished relating everything he knew about the accident and prayed with Cole, he gave him a long hug, and asked if he had any questions. Cole shook his head, no, and just sat quietly. Mike's heart hurt mightily, and he grabbed Cole and held him tight as both of them cried. Karen came in and put her arms around both of them.

Cole looked up at Karen. "Where is my dad right now?"

"He is on his way home, Cole." Mike said.

"When will he get here?"

"Sometime tomorrow, and you will stay here with us. We'll all stick together."

"Is my dad okay? Does he know about Mom?"

"Yes, son. I've told your dad what I told you."

"I know my dad needs me to be strong, and I will. I'll take care of him."

Mike could hardly hold it together. The courage of this young boy tugged at his heart like nothing he had ever experienced. Cole had always been much older than his years. Both Al and Cindy treated him like a little adult. They had instilled confidence in him and trusted him with responsibilities that some adults could not handle. He was a remarkable young man. He had heard Al pray over his son many times that God would grow Cole in His wisdom and lead him into eternal truths. Mike was confident God would carry them all in his resurrected and healing powers. His grace is sufficient.

—

Al had been driving most of the night when exhaustion took over his mind and body. He pulled over to a roadside park, killed the engine, cracked the back window of his truck, and fell asleep. A few hours later, he awoke with a start. For a moment, he could not recollect where he was, and then the pain and agony of his loss flooded his soul and clutched his heart to the point that he could hardly get a breath! *Oh, God, keep me sane, help me stay the course, carry me, dear Jesus, for I'm drowning in my grief. Please comfort my son, Father. Please help us both get through this horrible tragedy and persevere.*

As Al got on the road again, his thoughts took him way back. Back to the time when his actions left a little boy motherless. How did that affect the boy? How did the boy's father cope? How did they make it? *Lord, I pray that You carried them and renewed their spirits, and I pray that You will do the same for Cole and me. At least I know that my precious wife and daughter are with You right now. Ever to rejoice with no tears, no struggles, just living in Your glory for an eternity. Father, that is what truly comforts me more than anything else right now, and I thank You for giving me that peace, dear Jesus.*

Clay and Dixie had been inseparable the entire week of his visit home! The two family's activities were blended together from the moment Clay had asked for Dixie's hand in marriage. The Anthonys and the Samuels were even more bonded with the news that their children were getting married, and Clay's plans were to live in Calveston after he finished his graduate studies. The church fellowship was all abuzz with the news! And of course, Pastor Anthony had great visions of Clay being associate pastor of their church.

Belle had tried several times to further discuss with Clay all the things she must tell him, but he had assured her that for right now, he was perfectly okay, and things would come to light in the Lord's timing. She was amazed at his lack of curiosity, and yet, living in the moment had always been Clay's way. Somehow, she felt it was a coping or blocking technique that he had subconsciously established in his life at a very young age. After several days, she gave up trying to acquire private time with him, and just enjoyed the present bliss with everyone else. She, herself, must rely on God to make a way. After all He was in control of everything, and that thought gave her peace.

Little Laura reveled in her big brother as he took great delight in all the things she wanted to share with him. They rode Prince together several times, and he went into great detail about his love for horses and running the barrels when he was younger. Laura, of course, wanted nothing more than to be like her big brother. Belle adored watching her two children enjoy one another's company. This was a time of jubilee, and she just needed to live the moment, as her son did.

Allie joined her family at home for spring break. She had really wanted Clay to come back for a visit, but after he mentioned going home, there was no need to think upon such. Clay was an enigma to Allie. She had the strangest attachment to him, as though she had some claim on him. He was the first guy she had ever been remotely drawn to, and it seemed thoughts of him were a daily thing. There was definitely a connection. She was anxious to get back to school so they could spend more time together.

"Hey, Sis, how about Clay? What's going on with him these days?"

"He is visiting his family this week."

"Thought you may invite him back here for the week."

"I was thinking about it when he told me he was going home."

"Are you hung up on this guy?"

"Odd terminology, Alan."

"Well, you know what I mean, Allie."

"I do, and I really don't know how to answer your question."

"What do you mean by that statement?"

"Honestly, I have strong feelings for Clay, but I'm not sure they are romantic feelings."

"How do you think he views you?"

"Now, that is a good question. I have no idea."

"You know, he is an awesome individual. In some ways he is such a simple straightforward individual, and in some ways, he is mysterious and a bit complex. Does that make sense?"

"Very much so. Sometimes, when he is talking and baring his soul, I feel he is revealing profound and wise things, and on the other hand, he is revealing little about himself. Like I said, he is a real enigma."

"Have you shared these feelings with him?"

"You know, I've tried, but somehow the conversation will immediately change gears without my even knowing, and we're onto other subjects of interest. I just have to trust that God has his timing in all things."

"Point well taken."

Allie decided to run to her dad's office before lunch in hopes they could have some one on one time together. For some reason, she needed to be in his space.

John was surprised to see his daughter just pop into his office. It was such a pleasant surprise, though! Even though she had just turned seventeen, she seemed much older. She was definitely all grown up, and truly a beautiful woman inside and out. He was so proud of her, and her dreams. Whoever was fortunate enough to have her as a wife would be a very blessed man! He could not believe he was having such thoughts about his seventeen year old! Very confusing to a dad to have a child and a grown woman wrapped up in one person; yes, extremely difficult to digest.

"Hello Dad. Thought I would come by and take you out to lunch!"

"And it just so happens that I have no lunch plans today! Have you got anything specific on your mind, Allie?"

"Not really, Dad, just felt the need to be with you."

"Well, you'll be completing your first year of college soon. Are you still on target to complete your education at Moody?"

"Absolutely. I am plugged in and feel comfortable about my major. Actually I'll probably continue to take classes through the summers and graduate early. Hope that is okay with you and Mom."

"Why rush things when you are already enrolled in college a year ahead of your classmates?"

"My classmates seem so young and immature. I guess that's the way it has always been with me. Perhaps I was just born with an old spirit, reckon?"

"I reckon, honey. Your mom and I have always felt that you have lived in an adult world. For some reason, you never really reveled in your childhood."

"Hey Dad, you never talk about your first son, Eddie. What was he like? Was he more like Alan or me?"

"You know, Allie, I think about him all the time. His life could have been quite different if I had been married to your mom. To tell you the truth, I never took the time to get to know my son. I worked all the time, and the little time I did have at home was a moment to moment challenge with Kate. Whenever I think about Eddie, my heart will not allow me to linger in the past. I can only hope that he has a blessed life full of love and perhaps one day will find his way back to us."

"I'm sorry, Dad. This is not such a good subject for you. I'm always drawn to this picture you have of Eddie and his little dog. This is the only picture I've ever seen of him, and Nana and Papa have never displayed pictures of Eddie, either."

"I'm sure that is because they feel it would cause me more pain."

"Would it?"

"Probably."

"Wow, Dad, I have opened up your heart to more hurt. Can you forgive me?"

"Nothing to forgive. The truth sets us free, right? We must let God, our Father, draw us closer to Him through our trials and valleys. He can take what appears to be bad and bring good from it."

"You are absolutely correct!"

"Now, where are you taking me for lunch, young lady?"

—

Sleep seemed to elude Clay, even though he was exhausted from his flight's late arrival. He continued to replay the events of his visit home during the past week. New information surfacing, new direction for his future and also the thoughts of meeting with Allie and sharing his news. For some reason, he was not looking forward to telling her about his engagement to Dixie. He did not want to lose Allie. She was someone he felt he needed in his life, but was not sure in what capacity. At home he had seemed so sure of this new direction, and excited about making plans with Dixie, and now, things were not as clear. *Dear God, what do You want for my life? What are Your plans? Lord, what is it about me that I want to keep the door to my past closed tightly? I recognized that for the first time this last week, especially when Mom wanted to share details about my past. Details that were apparently painful to her, but nonetheless she felt necessary to relate, and I would not hear her out. What am I afraid of, Lord? Please help me unravel the things that keep me from walking in the truth about myself.*

—

Al dropped Cole off at school, and slowly drove back to the house. It was such an empty house. He could not seem to remember the good memories, the ones of love, laughter and spiritual blessings. Never had he experienced such agony in his life as he had the past week.

Mike and Karen had been remarkable in every way, and the church fellowship was incredible. Cindy and Molly's service was tender and in many ways a time of celebration because both were in the arms of Jesus together. He was glad that Molly's little body was placed in the arms of her mother. Somehow it was easier to think about them being buried together, even though it made little difference in a spiritual sense. Cole was his little man. He never left my side. He seemed to feel that I needed to be taken care of, and he was just the one to do it! Thinking of Cole in that light placed a smile on Al's face. Probably the first one since Cindy and Molly's deaths.

Richard James had called last night, and told Al that the corporation was in the process of purchasing a house for him in St. Louis, so he would be comfortable whenever he came into town on business. Al could not believe that his participation in the business was that important, since he had spearheaded very little in the last couple of months, and profits were soaring without his being involved. Perhaps it was just a small gesture of their kindness during this profound time of grief. Richard had also mentioned that the next time investors and managers met, there was a journalist from one of the prominent business magazines who wanted a personal interview with the founder of "Kingston's BEST."

To Al it seemed that life somehow carried one along, even in dark and lonesome times. Life just marches on at a great pace. There really is little time for a pity party and even less time for reflection when others are a major part of one's life.

Cole was Al's main focus, main motivation and his reason to go forward. He had to remain clear headed and give his attention to his son, the only family he had left in this world. *God, you will have to take my hand and totally lead me through this valley, Father. Give me a desire to get back into Your Word, and fill my mind with Your promises and hope. Keep me strong and give me the grace each day to have total acceptance of Your plan in my life. You are the Master, I am the clay; please carry me in Your peace and joy in and through this great gulf of pain. I need Your direction, not only for my life, but for my son's life. Father, I lay prostrate before the foot of the cross, pleading the blood of Jesus. Thank you, my Father.*

Clay and Allie had agreed to meet in their favorite spot under the familiar old oak tree after classes ended that afternoon. Allie had pondered about how to ask Clay to join their family for the birthday celebration of her grandmother, Esther. She hoped that he would want to come, but felt a bit uneasy about asking, since they had drifted apart over the last few months. Clay was hard to read in many ways, and on the other side of the coin, he seemed so straight forward in his approach to everything. At times she could not help but think there was a deep mystery embedded in his life, and perhaps one that even he was not aware of.

"Hey Allie, it is great to see you!"

Allie gave Clay a quick hug and asked him to have a seat beside her.

"Clay, it seems like it is been forever since we've visited! How are you and what's the latest?"

"Very busy preparing my thesis and keeping lessons prepared for YOUR class!"

"Won't be much longer until my class ends. I may not be seeing you much after that."

"Well, you know I'll continue my graduate studies through the summer, so we'll have many chances to visit."

"Speaking of visiting, how would you like to join us for a birthday celebration next weekend at our place? It is my grandmother's 75th birthday!"

"That sounds like fun. Let me check my schedule to make sure I do not have another commitment, and I'll let you know."

"Please do come, Clay. We all enjoy your company and Alan mentioned that he wants you to take a look at a horse he is thinking of purchasing. Of course, he would have to sell one of his horses in order to purchase another. It is a big decision for him, and his horses have become pets or more like family, so it will be hard for him to give one up."

"I cannot imagine giving up any of my horses. It would be like letting go of a family member for sure. Perhaps I could lend Alan some help on this matter. Actually, nothing comes to mind as far as my schedule, so unless I'm mistaken, I'll ride home with you next weekend for this special event!"

"Oh Clay, that is wonderful news! Not sure if I'll tell the family to expect their favorite guest or if I'll let your visit be a surprise! They are all so fond of you."

"I'm fond of them, too. I'm also fond of that fabulous carrot cake your grandmother makes . . . . it is to die for!"

"I bet she would make it just for you, Clay!"

"You think?"

"Yes! I can tell the way she looks at you, that she knows in her heart that you are a very special person."

"Don't know about that, but I do enjoy being with all of your family, and this will give me something to look forward to!"

"What about the visit with your family, Clay? How did it go?"

"Actually, it was the best time ever. There was so much family togetherness and my little sister Laura got to ride horses with me several times. She is growing up way too fast!!"

"Alan and I have talked a little about coming out to visit you one day and riding your horses, and seeing how a professional ranch is actually run. I think Alan would love that sort of life. He is desperately trying to find his niche."

"That is a great idea! Perhaps we need to try to make that happen sometime during the summer when I go back home!"

"Clay, on a serious note, you know how fond I am of you, and oft times I feel that we have a very special bond. There is something about our relationship I cannot define, and I wonder if you have some of these feelings?"

"Yes, Allie, the way you are describing our relationship is exactly how I feel. It is as though there is a spiritual connection that is indefinable."

"You know, Clay, I find myself praying for you all the time. It is as though the Spirit of God moves me to pray on your behalf."

"Allie, that is so comforting for I have many unresolved things in my life, and the older I get the more I discover I do not know, nor am I sure that I want to know. That probably does not make any sense to you whatsoever, but that is how I honestly feel."

"Life is a moment to moment experience, and God does not measure time like we do. You'll have plenty of opportunities to discover what God has for your life, and He'll lead you in His perfect Will, Clay. You are a man after God's own heart."

"Oh, Allie, I've said it before and it has to be said again, you are wise beyond your years. How I admire your intuitiveness."

"I could sit here and talk all night to you, Clay Samuels, but I've got homework assignments awaiting me. Hope you have no conflicts about next weekend, and I'll be in touch as to the time we'll depart for St. Louis, okay?"

Clay brushed her small slender hand with the tips of his fingers. "Okay, Allie, take care."

Dixie was basking in the fact that she and Clay would anchor their future in the community of Calveston. Her parents were excited and Belle and Les as well. What could be more perfect than to marry your childhood sweetheart and best friend. And that being the case, why was her spirit constantly in check? She just felt the impending dropping of a bomb. *Dear Lord, this is craziness. Please direct our every step and give us pure and lovely thoughts. Protect sweet Clay wherever he is and whatever he is doing.*

Belle's nights were hard times for her. All the demons came out and pulled on her in every imaginable way. She would be jerked back to the past with every accusation shouted to her up until the present time. She could never position herself in peace or safety no matter how she tried to stand on the promises of her Lord. If anyone could read her mind they would think she had surely lost it! She had even thought of asking Claire to keep Laura for her and keep an eye on Les while she flew to St. Louis and talked with the authorities about the day Clay's mom was killed. Would they believe her? Would they think she had killed Kate Marshall? What would this do to her family? What would it do to Clay? One choice in the past could change one's entire future. *My Dear Lord, You simply must guide me each step of the way. I want more than anything to walk in the truth. Please go before me and make all those crooked places straight, and as this impending storm shall without a doubt affect us all, keep us steadied and grounded in You, knowing that You will provide a way for healing and restoration for all of us. Oh, Lord, please let me walk in Your peace right now, and keep my thoughts from racing back and forth. Protect my family, and above all give us Your love to love and forgive one another.*

Al and Cole were nearing the street where their new house was located in St. Louis. Al could not believe the houses were so grand. He had let

Richard and the corporation handle things in the manner they deemed best, and really had not given much thought to their plans or questioned anything regarding his move. He knew that Kingston had to remain in the past or he would forever live in a graveyard. His grief for Cindy and Molly totally consumed him while he was there with Cole, and he could see Cole becoming withdrawn. Even though St. Louis held memories of a bad past, it was like that past belonged to someone other than himself. Jesus had totally renewed and restored him, so his past life as an unbeliever had been redeemed. He thought of St. Louis as a new start, new opportunities to get to know people and make a difference in their lives as he had in the lives of those dear ones in Kingston. He sold the Kingston home to Mike and Karen. They had outgrown their little home some years back. He was personally handling the financing for them. He also insisted that Mike take some shares of stock in the hardware business to insure things continued to grow. Mike needed a business link to the people in the community as well as being their pastor. It would give him a chance to better know the needs of the people and help them. Saying goodbye to Kingston was by far the hardest thing Al had done in his life. He just had to place Mayme, Cindy and little Molly in a treasured place within his heart, carry them with him at all times, but march to the drum beat of the future, not the past. Cole's whole life was ahead of him, and he deserved for his dad to have a clear head, hopeful heart and steadfast commitment to the Lord. *Lord, I'm Your vessel, I'm surrendered, and I need Your guidance every step of every day. Thank you, sweet Jesus. Thank you for my precious young man, who is so very brave. Go with us, Father.*

As Al pulled up into the driveway of their new home, Cole awakened from his nap, and yawned and stretched. Then his eyes became big and bright.

"Oh, Dad, is this our new place?"

"Yes, son, this is our new home. How do you like it so far?"

"How do I like it? I love it!"

"Well, let's hop out and go explore, okay? We'll let you decide first which bedroom you would like!"

"Dad, this is like no house I've ever seen. Are you positive this is our place?"

"Well, let's see if our key opens the door. I suppose that will be proof enough, right?"

Al slipped the key in the front door and gave it a gentle turn. When the door opened, they were totally taken aback not only by the warmth of the house, but beautiful arrangements of cut flowers were placed in the foyer, great room and kitchen, and as far as the eye could see the lighting and angles of their home was more than Al could have ever imagined. Cole leaped up the stairs looking for his bedroom. The first room he came to was a perfect fit for him. There was a set of beautifully carved oak twin beds, a well lit desk for studying with book shelves that went to the ceiling, and a fascinating aquarium that was at least half the size of a twin bed. It was built across from the beds where someone had given much thought to the mural on the wall behind it. It was a beautiful ocean scene that brought about tranquility to the spirit.

Cole ran into his dad coming up the stairs, and wrapped his slender long arms around his dad's waist.

"Hey, I hope these are tears of joy!"

"Oh, Dad, they are!"

"So, I guess this means you've found your room, right?"

"Yes sir, if it is okay with you!"

"Cole, you know whatever you want is fine with me."

"Okay, Dad, let's find your room!"

"I believe the room I would like is downstairs. Actually, I'm glad you are upstairs because it seems to be safer."

"What do you mean by safer, Dad?"

"Perhaps, I should have said more private. You'll have your own space, and I guess you saw the game room beside your bedroom, right?"

"I did, and you and I can play ping pong together!"

"Yes, that's right, and when you find new friends, you can have the entire upstairs for your space, and enjoy entertaining pals!"

"You always think of others, Dad. Did you know that?"

"That is the way Jesus works, son, and you of all people walk that path, too."

"Where is your room, Dad?"

"Downstairs and just past the kitchen. Guess who will be close to the midnight snacks?"

"Wow, this is enormous!"

The master bedroom was beautifully decorated, but very simple. Fresh flowers were on each nightstand, and there was a beautiful marble fireplace beside sliding glass doors going out to a rose garden with a fountain. The landscapers had done an impeccable job, and it seemed to Al that this was a little paradise. He knew many hours would be spent right here in the courtyard.

There was a guest bedroom down stairs, and a small loft on the third level where a beautiful sunroom had been designed with plants of every description and a small deck for viewing the starry nights and full moons.

It was rather staggering for Al to think that Kingston's BEST honey had enabled him to have a place so elaborate. Certainly, God had brought all the right people and professional marketing tools to his company. *God, sometimes, I lament that life is not fair, and perhaps it is not, but You, O, Lord, are just and merciful, and have designed the master plan for our lives before the foundation of the earth was formed. Father, I thank you, I am grateful, and I am so humbled. I want more than anything to continue to be Your servant, and give Cole the spiritual opportunities that I never had as a young boy. Merciful God, bless our home and protect us. May many souls be won for Your glory in this home.*

Al continued to be amazed at the compassion and thoughtfulness of the people in his company. Not only were the furnishings magnificent, but someone had taken great care to stock the pantry and fill the refrigerator and freezer with enough food to last the two of them several months. Al knew that Richard James not only was a prosperous and brilliant businessman, but a man of great wisdom and compassion. Everything about this house said volumes about Richard. *Lord, bless him, and continue to allow me to give others opportunities to better themselves and get to know You.*

Upon retiring that night Al reflected on the amazing events of the day. Just thinking about Cole's excitement, expressions and hopefulness was worth it all. Richard had called earlier that night, and asked Al if he could meet with Dana Fulton for a visit over lunch on Tuesday. She worked for "The Entrepreneur," a business magazine that wanted to write an article on "Kingston's BEST." Ms. Fulton was particularly interested to hear the facts about the company's meager beginnings, and the secrets of such a whirlwind success.

Al's thoughts took him immediately back to his low life when he was entangled with drugs and all the deceit involved. That's what it was, deceit! His life had been one huge lie. Sometimes he could hardly bear to think about the Marshall family, and his part in changing their lives forever. Yes, plenty of blame could be cast directly on him. In some ways his past actions would always haunt him, but in other ways God had redeemed and restored his life and blessed him beyond belief. When he thought about the loss of Mayme, Cindy and Molly, he felt a profound hollowness in his heart, probably the same as John Marshall felt about the loss of his wife and son. The first time Al returned to St. Louis after Kate Marshall's death, he had gone to the library and looked up all the past articles on the Marshall family. The part that still plagued him the most was the fact that the little boy was missing. *Dear God, I pray that You redeemed that child and grew him in Your image. I believe more than anything in this world, I should get the most relief from knowing that innocent child grew to know and trust You in all aspects of his life. Wherever he is Lord, bless him. Lord, I know from Your Word that it is the humble of heart who You bless with Your wisdom. I ask that you keep me stripped of any pride in my life. Let me live in a way that would serve Your Kingdom purpose, giving others opportunities to allow You to change their lives. Help me always remember that this is not my home, and only those things done for You will count in our eternal life, Father. Oh, Father, help me to be strong of faith, walk uprightly, and share Your love in all that I do.*

Allie and Clay stopped by John's law firm on their way home to Allie's grandmother's 75th birthday celebration. Allie had wanted to surprise her dad and everyone else with Clay's visit. She noticed that Clay's presence brought out the best in everyone, and she knew her dad was quite fond of him. Actually, she was really fond of him, but in all the time they had known one another, she did not sense that he was attracted to her. Theirs was a unique relationship, certainly a spiritual bond and a treasured friendship, but was that all?

Clay extended his hand to John Marshall. "It is good to see you, sir."

"What a pleasant surprise, Clay, welcome."

Allie hugged and kissed her dad. "I thought I would surprise everyone by bringing Clay to Nana's celebration this weekend."

"You've certainly accomplished that with me, Allie!"

"Clay, tell me about your life over the last few months since we've been out of touch."

"Well, Mr. Marshall, graduate studies have kept me focused and very busy. I did travel home on spring break to visit with my family, but other than that, it is the life of a student, who needs to start earning his keep very soon."

"And just what is it that you want to do with your life, Clay?"

"As soon as I graduate, I'll be going back to Calveston, and going in business with my dad as a rancher. There is also the idea that I can help in the ministry of the local church I've always attended. Not sure about what capacity, but definitely staying grounded in the Lord's work."

"Sounds like you have a good plan, Clay. I know your parents are so happy you'll be living close to home."

"Yes sir, both of them are thrilled, and my little sister, Laura, needs her big brother around. I plan to groom her for the rodeo circuit, and she is very happy about that prospect!"

"I hope you'll always feel free to come and visit us in the future, Clay."

"That's a promise!"

Allie struck up a conversation with her dad, and filled him in regarding her latest experiences and goals for the near future. Clay was taking this time to relax and take in his surroundings. Mr. Marshall was certainly a successful businessman, and it was apparent that he had a rich personal life as well. As Clay scanned the bookshelves, his eyes rested on a picture that made his heart race. It looked just like a picture of his dog, Barney; Barney with a little blonde headed boy. Could it be? No, of course not.

As Allie finished her conversation Clay felt compelled to ask about the little boy and dog in the picture. "Mr. Marshall, I could not help noticing the little lad with the dog in the picture on your shelf."

"You know, Clay, that is a story for another time."

Clay noticed that Mr. Marshall's expression changed dramatically.

"Of course, Mr. Marshall."

"Hey Dad, we're headed home . . . see you there soon, okay?"

"Right."

As Clay positioned himself beside Allie in the car, he noticed a single tear drop falling from her cheek.

"What's up, Allie?"

"Clay, you deserve to have your question answered about the picture in my dad's office, and the reason why Dad ended the discussion was because it is all too painful. You see, that little boy in the picture is my dad's son by his first wife. His wife was killed in their home while Dad was working, and his son was never found. The whole thing has always been a mystery, and apparently a burden that my dad will always carry. I believe he carries a heavy load of guilt, and somehow feels responsible."

After the initial shock of Allie's statement, the first thought Clay had was that of wanting to protect his mom. *Oh, God, how can this be? I need to know the rest of the story from Mom, and yet this is my family, here, as well. Lifetimes we've spent apart, and only by Your divine design have we been brought together. Oh, my, Allie is my sister, Alan, my brother, and I have grandparents as well. And my dad is still deeply broken. Lord, the only way everyone could have persevered is through YOUR STRENGTH. Oh, Lord, carry me one step at the time for I feel totally helpless. Jesus, help me.*

"Clay, is everything okay? You certainly have gotten quiet. Hope my dad's lack of response to you has not offended you."

"No, Allie, I completely understand. I'm okay."

That evening, Esther was absolutely in her glory with the family rallying and celebrating her. She was deeply moved that Allie's young friend, Clay, had joined them for her birthday event. Esther sensed there was something about Clay that had changed since his last visit. He seemed quieter, more reserved and perhaps somewhat preoccupied. He was such a handsome young man. Actually, he was a beautiful man. She just wanted to go give him a big hug and share words of encouragement. There was just something about this young man that captured her heart. And then it dawned on her once again, he reminded her of what their grandson, Eddie, might have looked like at this age. Why couldn't this be Eddie? *It could be, couldn't it Lord? Dear Jesus, why does my spirit ponder such, if this were not so? Oh, Lord, how we need closure regarding our lost child!*

Alan was elated to have Clay visit again, and insisted that Clay ride horses with him the next day.

"Alan, you mustn't pressure Clay. He will only be here a short time." Allie spoke rather firmly.

Clay spoke up and said, "Actually, I would love to ride, and the weather seems mild enough for it to be pleasant for the horses, too."

Allie dismissed things with a smile, but felt somewhat left out, especially since Clay was her guest. Oh, well, she knew there would be other times.

As Clay ate the carrot cake Nana had baked, the memory of a world far away touched his brain when his palate embraced the first delicious bite. Just a glimpse of a gathering at another table, but with John Marshall and his parents, and a young woman who he could barely make out in his mind's eye. A familiar taste can bring back another time and another life. His senses were awakening, and removing the block that had protected him from painful memories. He remembered his mother's neglect, he remembered his little dog Barney being lost, he remembered his dad's sadness, and he remembered the day that this nice lady came and took him away from his life of long ago. He wanted to embrace his dad and his grandparents. Oh, how he longed to tell Allie that he was her brother, never to be her lover. He had known for some time that her feelings for him were more than he could deal with, and yet he never spoke up. There was something that connected them, and now he knew. And Alan was his brother. He wanted to jump up and tell them that all the pieces of the puzzle had been found, but there was this grind in his gut regarding his mom. This information could place her in jeopardy or worse. She had kidnapped him! Oh, Mom, how did you live with all of this for so long? It must have eaten away at you every single day of your life. You sacrificed everything to protect me, and give me a good life. You owed me nothing and gave me everything. I've had a marvelous life, and I'll have no regrets. Somehow we'll all get through this. *My Lord, You and You alone are the only One who can right what has been wronged. I am depending on You to take us all step by step, and bring honor and glory to Your Name. Let us not walk in fear, but confidence in Your strength and wisdom, and to know without a doubt what is impossible for men is very possible for YOU.*

Alan showed Clay the time of his life. Their horseback excursions were sprinkled with much serendipity throughout the entire day. Alan shared all about his dream of buying this gorgeous spread about twenty miles out from the city, and becoming a horse breeder of show horses. Clay noticed that Alan was a natural with horses, and his desire to make a life as a rancher was so prevalent. God had given him a love for horses that revealed a path of remarkable talent . . . . a God given talent with so much passion. This was so very exciting for Clay as he began to think upon the possibilities of he and Alan doing something together right here in St. Louis. *God, that had to be Your thought, not mine. Where did that come from? Dad and I just recently spoke of my helping him in Calveston. Lord, please lead us all in Your Master plan, as I am somewhat conflicted at the moment.*

The next morning as Clay was having breakfast with his new family, he could not help feeling richly blessed, even amid his trepidations of the entire truth surfacing. He wanted to have total clarity on where God wanted him, where he belonged in the future. He was still excited about the future possibility of he and Alan having a ranch together!

"So, Mr. Marshall, what do you think of Alan's dream to be a rancher and breed show horses?"

"Well, Clay, I'm happy my son has this dream, but at the same time, I wonder how realistic the idea is when it comes to an income that could support one."

"I believe God opens doors to utilize the talents He gave us. He places dreams within us, and He will place us where we belong. I'm ever so confident He has the Master plan, and divinely designed every detail of our lives before we were born."

"It sounds good, but getting started, working through initial details and networking with the right people, sounds like something that is out of our league."

"I've been excited about this since Alan shared his dream and told me about the land that could be purchased initially, and I believe it would work! I would be more than willing to help Alan get it going!"

Allie squealed with excitement. "Do you really mean that, Clay?"

"Actually, I really do. I've not been this excited about future endeavors and a certain course of action in a long time!"

Mr. Marshall got up from his chair, and came around and shook Alan's hand and Clay's. "Since this seems to be a dream that both of you are led to do, I believe I could invest in the initial start up expense. It would be a privilege to see you two work together in something that you really enjoy! Alan, you have a couple of more years before finishing your degree, that is if you take courses through the summers, so that will give all of us some time to save and come up with a workable plan for this venture."

The whole family was elated for the rest of the morning talking through the details of Alan's plan. Clay and Alan would be perfect partners, and their personalities complemented one another, as well. Clay would keep Alan grounded, and Alan would add much enthusiasm to Clay's life!

Clay found himself much more relaxed around the Marshalls since learning that they were his family, his roots. It was so easy to love all of them, but he could not help wondering what their reaction would be when they learned the truth. He knew he would need to talk with his mom before revealing the entire truth to the Marshalls. He had many questions to ask his mom and his real dad. He realized that he needed to get home as soon as possible. Finishing his graduate studies would have to take a back seat for now.

"Mom, Clay just called and he is coming home for a visit before he finishes this semester!" Dixie blurted out.

"Well, that is a bit of a surprise, isn't it?" said Claire.

"You know, it certainly is. Wonder what's up?"

"Maybe he is missing you, darling."

"It will be heaven seeing him, but for some reason, I have a knot in my stomach."

"That's not like you, Dixie."

"I don't know, Mom, but I have a feeling something is astir."

"You and your intuition!"

"I need to stop by and see Belle. See how she is doing."

"I've not been a very attentive friend for Belle in the last few years with all the things going on here on the home front, and then assisting your dad with some of the tasks at the church. She probably feels neglected, and to think we use to be so very close, but children have a way of changing our lives."

"Well, I'm going to run on over and check on her, Mom, okay?"

"Be back for supper, right?"

"Indeed, I will, and I'll do the clean-up afterwards, Mom."

When Dixie stopped by Belle's, the first thing out of Belle's mouth was that Clay was coming home for a visit.

Dixie did not mention that she also knew. "Oh, Belle, aren't you glad Clay will be coming home for good later this year? I can hardly wait!"

"Do you really think that will happen, Dixie?"

"Well, why wouldn't it?"

"I'm just not sure Clay has really found his way yet. Something tells me he has unfinished business where he is now."

"What are you talking about, Belle?"

"Hasn't Clay related to you what I've told him about his past?"

"Not much, but yes, some."

"His biological family is somewhere in St. Louis, and if I know Clay, he will get to the bottom of all of this."

"So Belle, you feel like his future may be there?"

"At least for a while, Dixie.... I just know it!"

"Belle, let's remember that we have a big God .... much bigger than any problem we encounter. Shall we just live in the day, and trust him with all our hearts?"

"Of course, Dixie, we shall. Your visit was ordained by our Heavenly Father today. What a wise woman you are . . . . as wise as our Clay. We must always remember that it is God's agenda and He'll make a way for His divine plan to be revealed in His time."

Dixie went over and hugged Belle for a long time, trying to reassure her to take one step at a time, live to the best of her ability in the day that the Lord had given, and lean not on her own understanding. "Belle, we shall never know the thoughts and mind of God. They are incomprehensible, but we can TRUST our great God to not only deliver us, but fulfill all His promises."

"Again, your visit is a Godsend, Dixie."

"Hey, I smell chocolate cake! Isn't that Clay's favorite?"

"You bet it is! Shall we have a piece and celebrate? Our man is coming home!"

Dixie noticed throughout their visit that Belle seemed more relaxed, even giddy and carried on light-hearted conversation, something she had not seen in years! It was like she was witnessing a restoration of hope in sweet Belle. She had never in her whole life run across someone who loved her child as much as Belle loved Clay. Whatever bonded the two early on would carry them and keep them forever together. Belle loved her son from the very depth of her bone marrow. It was actually of a spiritual nature, and Clay was equally connected to his mother in the same way. Perhaps this bond of theirs all these years had been a survival mode for both. Dixie knew there would be grave changes for all of them when the entire truth surfaced.

—

Cole was doing great in school, and loved the fact that it was within walking distance of their home. Sometimes his dad would have business related appointments, and he could come home, get a snack and have his homework done by the time his dad arrived home. He loved their time in the kitchen at night. Each had their favorite cook books, and would take turns trying out new recipes of their choice! Cole tried hard to never be sad around his dad, but truth be known, he missed his mom so much, his heart felt that it would literally burst at times. He knew his dad probably felt the same way, so they both tried to be brave for the other.

Cole loved his new friends. He had so many more friends here than he had in Kingston. He had been much too busy in Kingston with domestic chores and church activities to really get close to classmates. He loved his new life, but longed for family.

"Is that you, Dad?"

"Sorry, I'm so late this evening, son, but I've been making notes so I'll be able to speak intelligently when I am interviewed by a journalist tomorrow."

"What are you going to talk about, Dad?"

"Actually, the whole interview is based on how Kingston's BEST honey grew into a successful business so rapidly."

"Because God blessed us, right, Dad?"

"That seems to be the best answer, yet! Would you like to go on this interview with me?"

"Could I, Dad?"

"I'll see if we can arrange just that!"

"Okay, little man, it is your turn to select what we'll be preparing for dinner tonight."

"Hot dogs, Dad!"

"You just want to make it easy on me, since it is late, right?"

"Actually, Dad, I want us to do dinner, clean the dishes quickly, and have a talk."

Al smiled at Cole and thought how grown up his son sounded. Many times he had thought about the wisdom God had instilled in this child. He was created in God's image, and was perfect in every way. He belonged to God. Borrowed for a very short time, and Al tried to always remind himself of that.

"Okay, son, what's on your mind this evening?"

"Do we have enough money to go anywhere we want to?"

"I suppose we do, and just where would you like to go?"

"Let's go out west and stay at a ranch, so I can learn how to ride horses. Dad, I love horses, and have never ridden one. Living in the city really limits my chances, don't you think?"

"Never thought about it Cole, since I've not had the opportunity either."

"Let's figure out a way for both of us to learn how to ride, Dad."

"Sounds like a great idea! I'll check around and see if we could get riding lessons together somewhere, okay?"

"Dad, that would be super! And then do you think we could take a trip out west and stay on a ranch? I would like a place where we could ride up in the mountains. Somewhere like Montana!"

"Gee, you have really put some thought into this, haven't you?"

"I've been thinking about it for some time now. I just want you and I to do some exciting things together, Dad."

"I'll check out our options, son, but for right now, it is time for both of us to get some sleep."

Al had asked Dana Fulton if she could change her schedule, and meet for dinner at their home in a more relaxed atmosphere, and that would give Cole an opportunity to be a part of the interview. After all, should anything happen to him, Cole would have 51% of the business. Ms. Fulton had gladly accommodated the schedule change, and was adamant about bringing over dinner for the three of them. Al and Cole had prepared a fruit pie from Mayme's hand written notebook of favorite things she loved to cook.

"I'll get the door, Dad!"

Cole opened the door, and to his surprise saw a beautiful lady with her arms overflowing with bags. "Come in, please, and let me help you with your packages."

"Why, thank you very much, and you would have to be the man of the house, right?"

"I'm the little man, and my dad is the big man!"

"Hi, Ms. Fulton, I'm Al Statham, and this young man is my son, Cole. It is a pleasure to meet you."

"Mr. Statham, I've been looking forward to this for weeks!"

"Come on in and lighten your load. We'll have a bite to eat whenever you are ready."

"Okay, now is a great time. Hope your appetites are as big as mine tonight!"

After serving their plates, it seemed to be the general consensus that the sitting area in the courtyard would be the most pleasant place since the weather was fabulous and a beautiful sunset could be enjoyed.

Dana was mesmerized by the design and angles of the house. Someone had put a lot of thought into this home, and the furnishings were so clean and simple, which enhanced the design of the home. From the moment she was met at the door by Cole, she felt totally comfortable. The dad was just as gracious as his son. She wondered where the mother was. There had been no mention of a "Mrs. Statham."

"Ms. Fulton, we've got a pleasant surprise for dessert. It is a family favorite, and Cole helped me prepare it."

"Mr. Statham, please just call me Dana. Would that be okay with you?"

"Sure, if you will call me Al."

"Well, okay, I'll try."

"Hey Cole, would you do us the honors, and slice up the pie, and bring small forks and napkins, too, son."

"Okay, Dad!"

Dana could not help but notice the respect that flowed between the two. They each admired one another, which was rare for parent and child these days.

"Oh, my, the pie is excellent. I mean fantastic. Would you be willing to share the recipe?"

Cole commented, "I knew you would like it, so I have the recipe written on a note card for you."

"Cole, has anyone ever told you that you talk and act like an adult?"

"A few times."

"I just have to tell you that your politeness would exceed anyone's expectations."

"Dana, I'm not sure his head will get through his bedroom door tonight!"

"Ms. Fulton, are you going to interview my dad tonight?"

"You know, Cole, I would like to think about this interview as a good old fashioned visit, and we'll just place my recorder somewhere in a corner, and later I will pull out the most appropriate and pertinent things, and write an article about the success of your dad's company."

"Dana, let's go inside for our discussion. I believe it will be more comfortable, and Cole and I will endeavor to share the story of how Kingston's BEST honey came to be such a miraculous success."

Dana positioned herself in front of Al and Cole in a small comfortable glider while the two guys sat beside one another with Al's arm draped around his son.

"Okay, let's just start at the beginning. How did you get interested in bee keeping, Al?"

"We had access to land that was full of clover, and good neighbors in the community who allowed us to place bee colonies on their land, as well. I initially thought it would be a good trade for Cole to learn, and give him responsibilities growing up. Amazingly enough, he worked harder at it than I did. I was pretty busy running a hardware store. Cole took on as much responsibility as we would give him, and always mastered things with the greatest of ease. He helped his mother with various chores, and sang in the choir at our community church, too. I would have to say Cole was the key individual in Kingston's BEST initial success."

"Cole, your dad sure gives you a lot of credit. What do you have to say about that?"

"We were a team, Mom, Dad and me. We could always depend on each other, and we also relied upon Jesus for daily guidance."

"You are telling me that you come from a Christian home, right?"

"Yes ma'am, I do."

"You mentioned your mom. Is she still a part of Kington's BEST?"

"In our hearts, she is. My mom and my little sister, Molly, were killed in an automobile accident. That was when we lived in the country in Kingston."

"Oh, my, I am so sorry. I did not know. I feel that I have gone way over my boundaries. Would you please forgive me?"

"There is nothing to forgive, Dana. Cindy will always be in our hearts even though she is not in our lives. We do not want to avoid talking about Cindy or Molly, but we both try to live in the present, so we will be making rich memories."

"Mr. Statham, you and your son have wonderful attitudes."

"Now, Dana, you must just call me Al. I'm just a country boy, not even remotely attached to the title I have been given in our company, okay?"

"I'm sorry. I will really try."

"Dana, I must share with you who really gets credit for the success of this company. You see, I believe only God could have brought all of this about. Early in my life, before I came to know Jesus as my Savior, I was on a dark and worthless path. I'm certainly not saying I did not know what I was doing, but for some reason I did not care, nor think about all the tragic circumstances caused by my choices and actions. By the grace of God, He placed in my path a Godly individual who shared the love of Jesus with me, and my eyes and ears were opened to a new way of living."

"So, you are saying your faith changed every aspect of your life?"

"Yes, in short, that is correct. God's guidance continually changes the course of our lives. He brought the attention of bright marketing people into our organization. There would have been no way this company could have expanded into the various markets without the talent of these visionary people. We have become diverse in the food market, the supplement market and just recently branched out into skin care products. The team that God brought together in our company continues to amaze me with their creative minds and innovations. Kingston's BEST honey started out as only a food line, and has over the last year become an organization with many connected businesses, all of which are extremely successful and profitable. I do not believe this was just by chance. I believe it was God's plan so He could ultimately reach out to many. It has been my philosophy to give the people who would have little chance of employment a real chance to know their self worth by employing them in areas where they can learn the business, buy shares of the business, and become part of a worthy cause. Actually, God led me along this path in my hardware business, and it changed lives in such a beautiful way that I keep looking for ways to bring good people on board who have never had much of a chance in life."

"Al, that is an awesome story. You are so selfless and genuine in your approach to business, big business, I might add."

"Dana, I truly believe this is God's approach. He is a God of second chances, you know?"

"Actually, I never really thought about it in this light before. You have an incredible story, Mr. Statham."

Clay had been busy planning his trip back home, and he and Allie had really had no time for a visit since their return to school. He planned to talk with her this evening in their favorite spot under the grand old oak tree. For some reason his stomach was in a knot. He suspected that her affection for him was misdirected, and felt he owed her an explanation. He was totally depending upon God to guide him through the rough times ahead, not only with Allie and her family, but with his as well. He was an integral part of two distinct families, and this was not the time for allegiance to one over the other. *God, I hand over all control to You. You can bring glory from what we perceive as a very difficult valley. You will have to lead me, Father. My heart faints and my knees tremble at the thought of moving forward in any direction right now. I place myself and my families in Your hands, precious Jesus.*

Allie ran up to Clay and wrapped her arms around him, gave him a kiss on the check, and patted the bench for him to have a seat. "Hey stranger! Haven't heard a peep from you since we returned! Guess that means you've been super busy with organizing things before you leave to visit your family, right?"

"That would be correct."

"Oh, Clay, I've thought about your visit with us, and all the possibilities that the future holds in your being a part of our family, especially your interest in Alan's dream and possible career!"

"Yes, I've been giving quite a bit of thought to the same, Allie."

"Clay, I do not know how to approach this subject, and perhaps the best way is just to be straight forward. Where do you feel that our relationship is going?"

"Allie, I know without a doubt, you will always be a part of my life, but I also know that we will not have a serious relationship that would grow into a permanent one, such as husband and wife. I realize what I just said sounds rather abrupt, but it had to be said."

Allie remained quiet with big tears dropping from her little chin. Clay's heart was breaking into a million pieces. *Oh, God, only YOU can work this out . . . calm our fears, ease our pain, and make something glorious out of these very complicated circumstances.*

"Sorry, Clay, for crying. Guess I've had the wrong idea for a while, and my imagination got carried away."

"Oh, my precious Allie, there is no need or reason to apologize to me. You had every right to wonder, and you deserve the whole truth and nothing but the truth. What I'm about to tell you will change many hearts and lives, and I humbly ask that you pray for God's guidance as you digest and share with others whenever you deem appropriate. Do you remember the other day when we were in your dad's office, and I asked about the picture of the little boy with the dog?"

"Uh, yes, I do, but what does that have to do with us?"

"This is very difficult, but I'm trying to get there. I have recently been told some of the details, but certainly not all, but I do know this. I am the little boy in that picture. I am your dad's son."

Allie's heart jumped right into her throat. She had known since the time she met Clay that there was some type of spiritual bond, and yes, this explained so much of what she had felt in her spirit from the very beginning, but of course, this was the part she had not chosen to ponder.

"Part of me is dumbfounded and part of me knew. Yes, Clay, I sensed something more than just an attraction to you. Even though it feels as if my world is falling apart right now, I'm confident God will get us all through this. I need to place my own thoughts and hurt aside, so we can approach the plan that God has for all of us. Oh, my dad. I can hardly begin to think about how this news will affect his life, and my grandparents' lives. Oh, Clay, all the rippling effects, some grand and some very difficult."

"Allie, I need to ask you a favor. Would you please try to keep this information to yourself until I've had a chance to get all of the details from my mom when I visit my family next week?"

"Oh, Clay, I just want to run to my dad and ease his pain. Absolutely, run to him, hold him and tell him everything is okay. How can you ask me to not do this?"

"Should the Lord lead you to do so, then let it be. I just ask that you be led of the Holy Spirit."

"Clay, you are my brother! It is so difficult for me to wrap my mind around all of this!"

"It is difficult for me, too, but in many ways, it is liberating and wonderful. The Lord has given me two precious families, and I love them, both. Allie, I promise we will talk through all of this and try to process things before I leave to go home. Let's plan to visit each evening and discuss the things that need to be talked about, okay? The things that we need to see clearly before embarking upon sharing with others. May this be done in God's timing and His way."

"Oh, Clay, I'll try."

—

As Dixie approached the gate at the airport, she could see the top of Clay's head above the crowd. He had that same broad smile and easy gait about him. Oh, how she loved this man! She had never seen him anxious, upset or rattled about anything other than his nightmares. Who can help what they dream, right? He was the most stable individual she had ever known. Only a person directed by God could have such a disposition, and he was hers!

As they drew closer, she could not help but run into his arms.

"Hey good looking! I have missed you so much, my beautiful woman!"

"Oh, Clay, it is wonderful being in your arms once again. How I wish we never had to part!"

"Hush, let's not go there right now, okay?"

"We've got lots planned for your visit. Knowing you, we'll take one day at the time, and you probably don't want the calendar details, right?"

"You know me well. Have I told you today that I love you?"

"Oh, Clay, I want to hear it every day!"

"I love you, Dixie, with ALL my heart."

"I love you, too, Clay. Oh, how I love you!"

"We have a whole week to catch up. Isn't that great?"

Before opening the door to the car, Clay pulled Dixie gently, but firmly against his body, and kissed her sweet lips and stroked her long black hair. They held on to another as though there were no tomorrow.

During their drive home Clay commented, "I'm ready to get married, Dixie, how about you?"

"Are you kidding or what?"

"Actually, I'm not kidding, but I realize it will take a little time to make wedding plans, so get started! Shall we have a Christmas wedding after I finish graduate school?"

"That sounds lovely. Do you suppose we need to share this with our parents this week?"

"Seems reasonable to me."

"Clay, have you given any thought to where we will live?"

"Here, for a while. Is that okay with you?"

"Here for a while, and then where?"

"Perhaps after a couple of years, I would like for us to consider a move to St. Louis. Would you be amenable?"

"The only thing I've ever thought about is living right here, but should you have career opportunities in another place, I will go where my husband goes. You know that, Clay."

"What more could a guy ask for? You are the greatest, my beautiful wife to be. You have made me a happy man!"

Clay's eyes glistened as he spoke softly to Dixie. She was without a doubt the woman God had prepared for him. *Oh, God, how can I thank You enough for all You have done for me, and to think if it had not been for my mom, I might never have met Dixie. There will always be good to come from our valleys, and God I know that You will be glorified in our union as a couple. We shall honor Your covenant marriage always. Thank you, sweet Jesus.*

"Look who is running to meet you!"

"Laura, sweetheart, come to your big brother! How are you doing?"

"We are all fine and so happy you are home! Mom has cooked all your favorite things and so has Ms. Claire. You are our favorite person in all the world, Clay!"

"Wow, what a welcome. Guess you are buttering me up to take you riding, right?"

"You are quite correct!"

"My, my, you are beginning to talk like an adult, little sister."

"That's what happens when you live around them all the time!"

"Listen to all of this, Dixie. What is your take on our little Laura?"

"Well, she is growing up fast . . . perhaps too fast or is time just passing us all by?"

When they approached the back door, Belle came out in a flash and wrapped herself around her big boy.

"It is so good to have you home, son."

"Mom, it is just grand to be here. Home sweet home."

"Hey Dad!" Clay grabbed his dad and gave him a big bear hug. "Both of you look terrific! Mom, I haven't seen you looking so rosy cheeked in a while . . . what's up?"

"Well, you know, son, I've been riding horses quite a bit with Laura and Les. Your dad has purchased a couple of new horses, and Laura and I are breaking them in!"

"Mom, I cannot believe you of all people have taken to horses. What's up with this?"

"Clay, we are totally a proper ranching family, now!" Laura announced.

"Where did this girl get her wit?"

"We can never get one up on her anymore. Your dad and I are always having to be on our toes around this young lady. She makes us dot all the "I's" and cross all the "T's" regarding any subject we broach!"

"Is this the gospel, Laura Samuels?"

"It is nothing but the truth, big brother!"

"Dad, I would have to guess that you are absolutely starving this time of day, right?"

"Yes, I am, but you were well worth the wait!"

"Okay, I say let's eat!"

After dinner Clay and Dixie slipped out to the back porch for some fresh air and privacy. There had been much talk at the dinner table about Clay coming back home to help his dad with the buying and selling of horses, plus lending his talents in the local church where Dixie's father was pastor. Dixie helped her dad with the financial end of things at the church and also wrote a weekly article in the San Antonio Sun. She had been saving most of her earnings from the last year, so this would help with housing or rent after she and Clay were married. Clay had been excited to share that the two of them were planning to have a Christmas wedding, and this pleased Dixie. It was really the first time both of them had felt free to show affection towards one another, and to share their plans regarding their future. Belle had been super charged. Actually, she seemed totally liberated from her usual guarded posture. She was full of humor and carried on such a healthy banter with everyone.

"Your mom amazed me tonight!"

"I agree, she was in rare form. Wonder what has made a difference?"

"Honestly, Clay, I believe she has finally come to terms with the past. And whatever music she has to face, I know God has prepared her, totally. She just has a peace that only Jesus could bestow."

"That's it. She has the peace of Jesus. Oh, my, what a difference. It has been a long time coming, hasn't it?"

"We'll never know the demons she fought for so many years. I cannot begin to imagine the guilt, fear, and self-condemnation. She is quite a woman. Certainly, not without fault, but one who has given up control. Yes, that's the difference – no more struggling for control of the situation."

"There is another element to this equation, too. She no longer feels the need to protect me. I'm confident she knows that whatever is ahead of us, nothing can change my allegiance to her, and the great love and respect I have and shall always have for her. I could not ask for a better mother, Dixie."

"I'm with you, there!"

"Sweetheart, there is so much I need to tell you, and I want to share it all with you before I sit down and have that long talk with Mom about all the grueling details of my past life. I feel the need to absolutely empty myself and receive wise counsel. Are you ready for a late night?"

"I'm with you from beginning to end, my love."

For the next three hours or so, Clay shared every emotion he felt regarding his biological family and all the things that had transpired throughout the year with each of them. Dixie did not say much, but she asked the right questions, so Clay could weigh things out from a more balanced perspective.

The story that Dana wrote for the editor of her magazine was without a doubt the most well received article she had written since being on board with the company. Her editor had called Al's company to secure permission for the St. Louis Herald to publish a similar story. From that story, much publicity came pouring into the marketing department of Kingston's BEST. There were so many inquiries, especially in the investment area. These articles had enhanced the business opportunities as no marketing strategy had ever promoted. For the first two weeks, the Personnel Department was busy installing new phone lines, and hiring help to answer the hundreds of new callers. Al was thrilled watching God bring more people on board. As requested, Al always received a copy of newly hired employees' background checks. There had been a few occasions where he would speak to the Personnel Director himself, and ask that certain individuals be given more opportunities to prove themselves in learning new skills, and advancing to a position that he knew would help them regarding their self-worth. Most of the time, he did not interfere with the running of the business. There were such capable people in the Personnel office, and his philosophy had always been well embraced during business meetings.

During the editing and fine tuning of Dana's article, she had visited with Al and Cole several times. Al always felt at ease with Dana, and Cole just adored her. During one of these visits, Dana talked about her family and love of horses. Cole just hung on every word. Her family lived in Montana and she had grown up riding horses. She shared many things about the big sky country and harsh winters. Life had not been easy for Dana's family. Everyone worked hard. Dana had two brothers who were still living at home. She had chosen to come east for her education, and loved the climate so much, she decided to stay. Her career choice was a good one, served her talent and provided an adequate living for Dana. She even volunteered to locate someone who could teach Cole to ride horses.

Al had been extra busy at the office lately, and felt a little guilty for not having more time with Cole. Thank goodness, he was not a high maintenance kid. He always seemed happy and full of interesting pursuits of his own. Dana had managed to find a place that boarded horses, and several of the owners had horses that could be rented by the hour for pleasure riding. She took Cole for his first horseback riding adventure, and that night during dinner, Cole covered every detail of his first experience riding a horse! It was amazing to Al how excited one could get when they had a passion about something. Cole apparently had thought about, perhaps dreamed about riding horses for some time before he shared his feelings. Al thought about his own life. He had never really had a passion about anything. Perhaps one's dreams create passion when one is young, loved and encouraged. He did not have such an experience. Yes, he was loved, but not nurtured in spiritual matters and healthy development. *Dear God, I would love to be passionate about something worthy. Do I have a real talent? Do I have any undiscovered dreams? Sometimes, there is a part of me that seems numb. Please take that from me and place Your vibrancy, Your enthusiasm, Your vision and Your passion within my spirit! Do grant that dear Lord!*

Cole was so pleased to have his dad come home from work early, and take him to the riding stables. This would be the first time his dad had seen him ride. He could hardly contain his immense pleasure! Ms. Fulton had taken off work several times to get him introduced to the basics, and now, she was traveling for the next two weeks. He had hesitated to ask his dad because the business seemed to pressure him lately, but finally he decided he needed time with his dad, and that was that!

"These are the stables up ahead to the right. Isn't it a grand place with the white fence bordering both sides of the road?"

"Yes, son, it is."

"Dad, you'll have to help me just a little in getting my horse saddled up. I can tote the saddle, but cannot get it on my horse."

"I believe we can take care of that."

"Hey Dad, are you going to ride with me today?"

"Tell you what, I'll plan to wear some blue jeans next time, and make an attempt to mount one of these handsome animals then. Will that be okay?"

"Terrific, and I bet Ms. Fulton could help you out!"

"You really like her, don't you, Cole?"

"Maybe love her, Dad!"

"Oh, my, I did not realize you were getting so attached."

"Dad, she is perfect in every way, and so very kind and interesting, too!"

"I see."

"Okay, now, you must give me a boost up into the saddle, and lead 'True' out to the corral."

"That's a good solid name. How did you come to select this horse to ride, son?"

"It was Ms. Fulton's choice. She talked to the owner about his temperament, and decided he would be a safe horse."

"She certainly thought of everything!"

"She is the greatest! Okay, now, watch me, Dad. First, I will get him into his gaits, then I'll have him gallop."

"Talking Greek to me now, but proceed, I'm watching with great anticipation!"

How thrilling it was to watch his son ride! Cole had accomplished much in such a short time. He looked happier than he had ever seen him before. After riding for about thirty minutes, Cole rested True and stroked his neck and talked to him. If Cole desired to continue to ride, perhaps a place out in the country where he could have his own horse should be a consideration. *Lord, I only want to be grounded in You, so wherever You want us and whatever You desire for our lives, just lead us through Your Holy Spirit. It is Your agenda, Lord.*

—

Belle had saddled up the new mare Les bought and rode out to the far side of their place, dismounted, and sat in the cool under a grand live oak. She took the bridle off Gypsy, attached a rope to her halter, and gave her freedom to graze in the foot high clover for a few minutes. She wanted to reflect on the wonderful time she had when Clay spent a whole week with them. He was the happiest she had ever remembered. Not that he had ever been unhappy, but he seemed liberated in his spirit. Yes, that was it. His passion for Dixie was so evident and he was quick to laugh at Laura and all of her antics. It was just a light hearted time for everyone. Even when she talked in depth with Clay about their entire past, he had a peaceful resolve about everything. They had talked and speculated to some degree what the future could present regarding unknowns, but both felt the peace of Jesus, and they both felt confident that God's hand was working to bring glory unto Himself. *Dear Lord, I have told my son everything, and now I ask that You give me the courage and Your strength to share all of this with my sweet husband. I need his support in order to go back to St. Louis and tell the authorities all I know regarding taking Clay from his family so long ago. I have to go back, face the truth and whatever consequences may befall, so I can go forward in Your Perfect Will. I'm not afraid, for I know that You will bring good out of all of this. I do ask You to help my husband and sweet daughter to forgive me and love me through all of this. And I ask these things in the precious Name of Jesus. Amen.*

Later that night after Belle had once again told her story in its entirety to her husband, she felt more liberated in her salvation. She and Les had decided to tell Laura a modified version of the facts, since it was doubtful she could comprehend the whole scope of things. Les was in favor of going with Belle to St. Louis as soon as they had a chance to sit down with Dixie and her folks. Laura would need to stay home, and perhaps Dixie could stay with her, and keep things as normal as possible during their absence. There were so many unknowns regarding the amount of time they would be gone, and they were concerned with the expense of such a trip, too. Both knew that God would provide, though. This was going to be a leap of faith on the part of everyone.

As Belle snuggled close to Les, she realized that she was closer and more united with her husband than ever before. *My precious Lord, keep us together, always. Les is so stable. He has been such a rock in my life. Please keep us both focused on You, and be our strong tower in these times of uncertainty.*

After Clay returned to school, he and Allie had talked non-stop for a couple of weeks. He had asked her every question he could think of regarding their dad. They had talked extensively about their grandparents and Alan, too. Clay told Allie many details about the life he had with his family. She responded many times with tears and a sweet smile.

For Allie, it was difficult listening to Clay proclaim such a deep love for his family. There was a part of her that resented the fact that her father never had an opportunity to share life's experiences with Clay. And she nor Alan had had a chance to know their own brother. Even now, it was hard to enjoy their present fellowship because of the entanglements of the past. Every time she thought about her dad learning that Clay was his son, she felt a wave of nausea. At times, she wanted to run straight to her dad and tell him the great news. His son who was lost, has now been found. And then her heart would ache for all the lost years. For her dad they were years of guilt, torment and a broken heart. She knew they would get through all of this, and she also knew there would be much joy to override the pain. If she could only fast-forward, and start a new scene in six months or so. *Dear God, You know how heavy my heart is. I hurt for my entire family. Please help me to not think ahead, but just be still before You, wait on You to guide my steps. Your ways and thoughts are always higher than ours, so I do not ask for understanding regarding all my questions, but a gentle and peaceful acceptance of what shall be. I covet the leadership of the Holy Spirit. Oh, Father, I beg of you to prepare the hearts of everyone in both families. Let this be worked out in Your order and design so You will receive glory, Father.*

"Oh, Allie, you continue to be so hurt from all of the past surfacing. My heart aches because your pure heart is breaking. Your life has always been abundantly blessed in every way, and I know that I've brought you so much pain. I have had my times where the flesh takes over, and I cannot imagine how all this will work out, and then I'm reminded that we have the opportunity to operate in the peace of Jesus, when we give all control to Him. Operating in the flesh will always take us to those places of fear and anxiety. Perhaps we need to pray together when our emotions start taking over. My mom called yesterday, and she and Dad are flying into St. Louis day after tomorrow. I really need to finalize a few things here before meeting them, so I may not have time to talk much the rest of the week."

"Why don't you let me drive you to St. Louis this weekend? My friend, Jen, is always so gracious to loan me her car. It will be much better than taking the bus, and quicker, too."

"How do you think you'll feel at home, now? Won't you be plagued and pulled regarding sharing all of this information with your dad?"

"I'm quite sure I will, but as you said, we will give this to God, and He will lead us."

"Okay, Allie. Thanks for the offer. We'll go together."

"Clay, I will do whatever I can for you. You are part of all of us."

"Thank you, Allie, for being so understanding. We'll make it, I promise."

Al, Dana and Cole had just returned from riding horses at the stables, and this had been the first time Al had ridden a horse. He had to admit, it was exhilarating and tremendously satisfying to be involved in an activity as such with his son. Cole had become an expert rider in such a short time. Dana had devoted much of her time in helping Cole not only learn how to ride well, but educating him on every aspect of a horse's nature, needs and peculiarities. Dana was a natural in the saddle. She had mentioned to Cole that she would be going home to Montana for a long week-end, and he was welcomed to come along and ride in the mountains where their family ranch was located. This had thrilled Cole, but given Al quite a bit to ponder and pray about. He did feel comfortable with Dana being responsible for Cole. Her family hosted youth groups every summer, and this would be an excellent experience for Cole to interact with kids his age in a setting that would be exciting for him. His son had not been away from him since the death of Cindy, and he wondered how he would manage without him. Dana was becoming such an important part of their lives, but Al still found himself feeling unworthy and undeserving to even entertain thoughts of having a permanent relationship with anyone. Thinking back, he hardly remembered how he could have ever thought himself worthy of Cindy. If it had not been for Mayme's intervening, he and Cindy would not have been acquainted, and certainly not married.

Al knew that people saw him and judged him in light of his perceived status and success. He saw himself, not only as who he was, but who he had been. Why couldn't he look upon himself as who he belonged to? *Dear God, I know I am Yours, and righteous because of Your Son, but sometimes I have a hard time looking at myself as redeemed. Lord, I need specific guidance in every detail of my life. If any Kingdom purpose is to be fulfilled by Dana being in our lives, please give me clarity, and Lord, keep me humble in all things, so I may have the favor of Your wisdom.*

"Hey Dad, are you still considering letting me go with Ms. Fulton to Montana?"

"Now, Cole, do you really think this is a fair question to ask me in front of Dana?"

"I guess not, but don't we need to make flight reservations ahead of time?"

"True, you have a point. Okay, I'll give Dana the money for your flight, and we'll plan toward your going. I'll give you a definite answer over the week-end."

"Oh, Al, he'll have such a good time, and perhaps you could use this time to finish up your scheduled meetings with your marketing managers."

"Sounds good, Dana. I'll give you my answer on Sunday. That will give you both plenty of time to pack up, and fly out on Wednesday, won't it?"

"Indeed. Thanks, Al."

"Hey Dad, could I take our camera along?"

"Sure, we'll need plenty of pictures of those gorgeous mountain ranges and majestic sunsets. Who knows, I may go along next time!"

"We may end up living out west after all, right Dad?"

"Just never know about us, son!"

As Belle and Les arrived in St. Louis, Clay caught sight of his mom at the gate and ran to embrace her. He picked her up and swung her around. Les came up and joined them, placing his arms around both his wife and son. He loved Clay more than ever, and considered him such an honorable man. His life had always been wrapped up in these two, and he had to keep pushing down his fears and anxieties concerning all the unknowns they were yet to encounter.

Allie stepped up and stood beside Clay. "Hello, I'm Allie, Clay's sister."

Clay moved close to her. "Mom, Dad, this is Allie, who you've heard so much about."

Belle could see the remarkable resemblance between the two. No doubting that the two were related. "Hello, Allie. We are so pleased to meet you, and I know this must be not only difficult, but terrifying in some ways to meet the person that abducted your brother so many years ago. I am so sorry, Allie."

"Mom, please, we'll get through all of this, I promise. Don't cry, it's going to be okay."

"Ms. Belle, please do not feel uncomfortable. Clay and I have been over every detail, and I know God will get all of us through this."

"Oh, Allie, you are so very kind. Thank you."

"Mom, Dad, why don't we go talk over dinner. Allie knows where there is a quaint little restaurant where the booths are rather private and we can get a bite to eat, and have a chance to talk things out. Does that sound okay?"

"Sure, son," Les said, placing his arm around Clay.

"Allie, why don't you and I go get the car out of parking, and drive by the baggage area and pick up Mom and Dad?"

"Okay, we'll see you shortly," Allie quickly stated.

As they were walking to the car, Clay could not help noticing the tears streaming down Allie's face. "Sweet Allie, I'm sorry this is so hard on you."

"It is horrible, Clay. Seeing you call them Mom and Dad, and your dad calling you son, and just seeing the love all of you have for one another. I can't help thinking about what all of us missed by your not being part of your real family."

"Allie, I'm so sorry, so terribly sorry. Please don't hold anything against my parents. Why don't you drop us off at the restaurant, and perhaps go join the family at home. We'll catch a cab to our hotel. I honestly think it would be easier for you."

She cried even harder, and he knew without a doubt this would be the hardest thing any of them could ever go through.

"Yes, I know you are right, I'll do that," Allie sobbed.

—

Sitting at the restaurant and picking at her food, Belle felt totally overwhelmed. She had seen the deep hurt in Allie. This was Clay's sister. Now thinking about how his real dad would feel, she could hardly hold herself together. She could feel herself withdrawing, and settling into a numb stupor. It was good to know that Les and Clay would take care of things, and she knew they would do and say the right things. She just wanted to go away. How could she have thought any of this would possibly work out? She could not bear to think about anything right now.

"Son, Allie seems so genuine, and I can see you care deeply for her, as I'm sure you feel for your father and brother. Belle told me that you had also gotten to know your grandparents. Trust me, we'll get through all of this one step at the time. It will do no good whatsoever to speculate or try to figure things out ahead of time. God will carry us through each moment, and comfort us and guide us with His Spirit."

"I know what you are saying is nothing but the truth, but dad, it is so very difficult to see those you love crushed, broken and wounded. I would give anything to take all the pain away."

"Clay, that is what Jesus offers to do when we allow Him to carry us in His peace."

"Easier said than done, though."

Les softly spoke, "Tonight when we get to our hotel, we need to read the Word together, pray together and give everything to God. He wants us to totally trust Him, and the only way we'll come close to honoring His wishes, is to stay in the Word and on our knees."

"Dad, I totally agree. Hey Mom, are you okay?"

Belle just sat quietly and slowly nodded her head, yes.

"Mom, tomorrow when we go to the authorities, I want you to let me speak on your behalf. I don't think you are up to taking the lead on this. Between Dad and me, we can share most of the details about what happened, and if there is anything of importance that you feel would clarify things, then certainly speak up.

Again, Belle just nodded her head and stared through hooded eyelids.

"Come on, son, let's get your mother to the hotel. She is in need of a good night's rest before we face the challenges of tomorrow."

—

When Allie walked through the front door unexpectedly, her mom ran to embrace her.

"Darling, it is wonderful to see you, what a surprise!"

Immediately, she knew something was dreadfully wrong with her child.

"What is it, Allie?"

Allie fell into her mother's arms and wept uncontrollably. She tried to speak, but was overcome with great gasping gulps of hysteria.

Anna shouted for John to hurry. She led Allie to the couch and helped her sit while wrapping herself around her fragile daughter. She could not imagine what awful thing had happened.

"Allie, my precious baby, what can I do? How can I help? Please be okay, sweet child."

John came running from upstairs in a panic.

"Anna, what on earth is going on here?"

"I don't know, John. She cannot catch her breath to speak."

"Allie, sweet child, nothing can be this bad. I've been through some pretty tough valleys, and God carried me, and He shall carry all of us now no matter what. Calm yourself, just sit quietly until you can breathe."

John and Anna held their precious daughter, and felt all of her brokenness and vulnerability. Even without knowing what was grieving her unduly, both of them were destroyed by this severe display of heartache. There was a deep rooted feeling in John that he was not going to be able to fix his daughter's heart.

Finally, Allie lay quietly on the couch. Anna went to get something for all of them to drink, and John just sat and prayed. Even though he did not know how to pray or what to pray for, he prayed hard.

"Dad, what I'm going to tell you, will bring you and our family reason to be joyful on one hand, but on the other, will most likely rip your very soul out of you."

"Allie, I cannot imagine, but I do know that whatever it is, I believe we will find strength in getting through this together. It is tearing you apart to carry this burden alone."

Allie broke down once again, and John moved to the couch so he could hold her. Anna came in with warm drinks and homemade cookies Nana had made that afternoon.

"Oh, my, we have regressed again. It is okay, sweet girl. Let's talk, Allie. Out with it, you cannot carry this alone any longer."

"Dad, Clay is your son."

"I don't understand. What are you saying?"

"Clay is Eddie, Dad. Haven't you felt at times after meeting Clay that there was a connection? I did many times, but chose to ignore it, because I was falling in love with him."

John tried his best to compose himself. "How did you come by your information, Allie?"

"The last time Clay visited, we stopped by your office, and he saw a picture of himself with Barney. He questioned you about who was in the picture, but you would not talk about it, so we discussed it when we got in the car."

"This is unbelievable. Are you certain this is the truth?"

"Oh, yes, Dad, I know this to be the truth."

John and Anna sat speechless.

—

Al had carefully followed the headlines each day for over a week regarding a woman named Belle Hamilton Samuels, who came forth on her own to admit to the kidnapping of Eddie Marshall some twenty years ago. There was to be a hearing on Friday in Judge Ray Lewis' court. The D.A. was building a case against Samuels in conjunction with the murder of Kate Marshall. Al had called Dana, and asked if perhaps she and Cole could extend their visit in Montana for a few days, since he had some immediate things to address. He had told her he would reimburse her of all expenses, including any income she may have to forfeit. Dana had been happy to help, and mentioned that Cole was thrilled to have a chance to vacation longer on their family ranch. With the most pressing things taken care of, Al pondered, prayed and buried himself in the scriptures. Yes, he could think of every reason in the world, especially things pertaining to Cole, why he should wait and see how things took shape regarding Belle

Samuels' innocence, but there was a constant nagging in his heart that this could be the very way God wanted to help him be liberated from his awful past. Hadn't he known that the truth would be revealed one day? His main concern, of course, was who would take care of Cole and guide him in spiritual matters. *God, You, and You alone, provide for Your children, and I know you'll make a way for Cole. I must rest in the knowledge that YOU are my defense, and I need no other.*

—

Clay was uncertain if his course of action was the right one, but he felt at this point, he had said and done all he could on his mom's behalf, and needed to visit with his biological family. He had not left his mom and dad's side since their initial visit with the authorities. Allie had come once to speak with him, to tell him that the Marshalls were not filing charges against Belle. He supposed that was a good thing, because the D.A. certainly did not need more ammunition! Since this case involved murder as well as kidnapping, the newspapers had gone to the extreme with speculations and accusations. His mom had been totally withdrawn from everyone the last two days, and only Les seemed of any comfort whatsoever to her. All of them had been instructed to stay in the city. His mom and dad had only left their hotel room to eat their meals. *Dear God, please comfort my mom and let her know she has not been abandoned by any of us nor You, sweet Jesus. Even though this whole situation looks grim at the moment, help each of us to know that You are totally in control of every detail. Lord, I ask that You help me to connect in a healthy way to my biological family. Please help each of us to walk in Your truth, and keep us connected with Your love as we all endeavor to work through the grief, regret and pain of the past. More than anything, I ask that you carry each of us in Your joy, so we can give and receive Your mercy and love. Thank you, precious Savior.*

Clay stepped out of the cab in front of the Marshalls' house. His breath was short, and his heart was beating fast and hard. *Help me, Lord.*

Allie ran out to meet him. "Clay, I'm so glad you came. Everyone, including my grandparents are more than ready to welcome you with open arms!"

He breathed a big sigh of relief, and placed her small hand in his.

John was standing at the front entrance, smiling with tears in his eyes. Clay stepped away from Allie and ran to his dad. Both men embraced and wept. Allie thought her heart would burst. She knew this would be one of the most emotional days any of them would ever experience. *Thank you, God, for bringing my father's son home.*

John ushered Clay into the living room where their family waited with open arms to welcome him.

Nana Marshall embraced Clay with all the love and warmth a grandmother could offer, and Papa Marshall grabbed him in a big bear hug. Alan could hardly wait to grab his hand and pull him to his chest, and dear gentle Anna smiled and hugged him close.

"I hardly know what to say," Clay mumbled wiping the tears from his face.

John grabbed him again, and broke down. Clay supported his dad and guided him to the sofa. Everyone found a chair and sat quietly until John composed himself.

Clay took a deep breath, and tried to speak of the things he knew his family wanted to hear him say. "I want you to know that I love each of you, and look forward to our spending more time together in the future. There are still many gaps in my memory, and at this point, I'm not sure if that really matters. What matters to me is that we are in one another's lives, and our great God will carry us beyond some of the pain we are presently experiencing. We will be building a new life together in the Will of God."

"You are right. We must build a new life together," John said.

"I'd like to start by calling you Dad. And Nana and Papa, you are wonderful grandparents. Right now, I feel abundantly blessed to be home."

John broke down once again. "I know this will pass, and only the rejoicing will remain, but right now, I just cannot get a grip on myself. There have been so many years of wondering and agonizing over our loss, but at the same time, we never quite gave up hope."

"Hey Dad, I'm here and I'm not going anywhere."

―

Belle could no longer think nor be further humiliated. The Assistant District Attorney had asked her every imaginable question regarding Kate Marshall's murder. The facts as she knew them had been related, and her mind was exhausted, her emotions depleted, and her heart felt hollow. Yes, she had reached the end of herself, and whatever penalty she had to pay or time she may have to serve was okay. She had turned it all over to God, and no longer could think in terms of past or future. She just wanted to be still and quiet and let the peace of Jesus pour over her entire being. *Dear Lord, I give thanks and praise to You for my devoted and faithful husband, my best friend. As he does his best to comfort me, I beg You to comfort us both and give us total assurance that trusting in You is all that is required of us at this present time.*

Al read the morning headlines, knelt beside his bed and prayed, then showered and dressed for the day's events. He knew without a doubt what God was calling him to do. He must sacrifice his all for another. He had placed everything in his life that was meaningful on God's altar, and now he would do his best to accomplish this mission that would undoubtedly change the rest of his life. Unknowns were not frightening; he had experienced his share of fear, and long ago given the burden to his Lord. *This will be the "DAY OF THE LORD" for He walks before me, and I shall not be afraid. You, Oh Lord, are my strong tower and defense.*

Judge Ray Lewis was a man of medium height and blue eyes. He calmly looked at each individual in the courtroom, as though he were surveying every heart. He had thoroughly read all the documentation given to him by the District Attorney's office, and had to admit, Mrs. Samuels needed to secure an attorney on her behalf.

Belle, Les and Clay were seated together on the front row, and John Marshall sat alone on the opposite side of the courtroom near the back. The state's two attorneys sat on the front row across from Belle. There was an officer and a stenographer sitting in chairs near the state's attorneys. The room was imposing, and every small movement or vibration was echoed throughout the entire courtroom.

"Mrs. Samuels, I would like to ask you a few questions here this morning before determining our next step in this case."

There was a distinct click heard from the door closing as someone entered the room. Judge Lewis took notice when the man had a seat in the back of his courtroom. All other eyes remained on the judge.

Judge Lewis continued, "Mrs. Samuels, it is my opinion after viewing the documentation I've been given from Officer Nelson and our state attorneys that you will need someone to defend you. Have you appointed an attorney on your behalf?"

Belle spoke so softly that Judge Lewis could only read her lips. "No, your Honor."

John Marshall stood and addressed the judge. "Your Honor, my name is John Marshall, and I will be glad to offer our firm's assistance in Mrs. Samuels' defense."

"Mr. Marshall, in light of your connection with the case, I don't believe this would be an acceptable solution, but I thank you for your kind gesture."

The judge looked at Belle with kind eyes. "Mrs. Samuels, even though there are no kidnapping charges held against you, there are certain facts the state must know regarding the death of Kate Marshall in order for this case to be closed."

"I understand, your Honor."

The man in the back of the courtroom stood and addressed the judge.

"Your Honor, if it would please the court, I would like to have permission to speak and clear up any charges held against Mrs. Samuels in this case."

"Sir, would you approach the bench?" Judge Lewis calmly said.

Al stepped away from his seat and walked up to the front of the Courtroom.

Judge Lewis immediately recognized this man to be the much publicized business mogul he had read so much about lately. What in the world could he possibly know about this case?

"Please tell the court your name, Sir."

"My name is Albert Statham."

"You have permission to speak, Sir. Take your seat in the witness stand, and share with the court what information you have that would release Mrs. Samuels from being indicted."

"I killed Kate Marshall."

The court was totally silent.

"Continue, Mr. Statham," Judge Lewis instructed.

"Some twenty years ago, I delivered drugs for a drug dealer here in St. Louis. On several occasions Kate Marshall bought drugs. The last time I saw her in her home, she was desperate for more drugs, but I was not delivering. She was extremely upset upon hearing this news. She pulled out a large knife from the kitchen drawer and lunged at me, making a couple of surface slices on my right flank. I tried to turn the blade away from myself, and the knife penetrated the left side of Mrs. Marshall's stomach. I could see the wound was not deep, but she bled out so quickly, and was gone. I have realized since then, I should have stayed, but at that time in my life, I knew that the authorities would never believe that her death was an accident. So, I ran."

"Mr. Statham, I'm not sure if the people of this court know that you are no longer dealing in drugs, but a successful businessman. For the records, please share with us how you arrived at the decision to bring this information to court today."

Al shared a personal account of his life, and when he finished all hearts had been touched.

"I would like to call a short recess. I expect everyone back here in this courtroom in one hour, 1:00 p.m."

—

Belle all but collapsed when she stepped outside the courtroom. Les and Clay led her to a bench close to a large window where the sun was shining brightly. Clay went in search of some water for his mom, and Les wrapped his arms around his fragile wife.

Al walked over to Belle and Les. "I'm so sorry, I've waited twenty years to reveal to the authorities this hidden knowledge. Everyone's lives could have been lived out differently, and perhaps with less pain and anguish, but in it all, our heavenly Father has brought about good things and Glory unto Himself."

"Only God could have given you the courage to do what you've done on my behalf."

"Mrs. Samuels, it was not just for your sake, but it was for my sake as well. I so desperately need the spiritual freedom, so I can be freed from the torment of my past, and allow God to take charge of my future, regardless of the consequences I must pay."

Belle could relate perfectly to what Al was saying.

Al quietly disengaged from the conversation, and walked down the hall to get some water.

John sat quietly in the courtroom pondering all that had been brought to light. Things he had wondered about for twenty years had come to light in less than an hour's time. Amazing how the truth really does set one free. Still he had a lot to work through regarding Eddie's kidnapping. There had been so much he missed. *Dear Lord in Heaven, let my final days be as Your servant, Job's. You blessed him and brought about total restoration in his soul from all of his losses. Oh Lord, give me Your love and mercy, so I may forgive and move forward, and I ask that You have mercy on all of us, Lord.*

Judge Lewis had never witnessed a hearing such as this one. In his years of serving as a judge, this was the first time a case had been reopened after so many years had passed. He knew that Belle was innocent, and he suspected that Albert was being truthful. The people were howling for somebody's blood, though. Mr. Statham would have no trouble paying a top-notch lawyer to defend him. Perhaps it would be a short trial, satisfy the crowd, and Statham would only have to pay a few fines for selling drugs twenty years ago. Twenty years ago . . . . look at this guy now.

—

Everyone was quietly seated in the courtroom, and Judge Lewis had instructed the stenographer to adjust the blinds. Apparently, the glare was obstructing his view. After another couple of minutes of silence, Judge Lewis asked the stenographer to approach the bench.

"Do you see how blinding the glare is in the back of the room? I need the blinds tilted upward so I can plainly see the faces of everyone when I address the court."

"Your Honor, I'll try again."

Judge Lewis rubbed his eyes, and then stretched them to open wider. There seemed to be some type of glare where Mr. Statham was sitting.

"Mr. Statham, there is a glare obstructing my view of you, kindly move to the other side of the room, please."

Al rose and walked to the other side and took his seat.

What the judge now saw were seven glowing outlines of what he thought to be angels. Yes, that was the only explanation. There was one very bright angel glowing all around Mr. Statham, and three dimmer ones on each side of him. They moved slightly as though being blown by a gentle breeze.

Everyone in the courtroom started getting restless as all eyes were on the judge, and his distraction.

"Ladies and gentlemen, I have weighed out the facts as they have been documented, and I have listened not only to the words of Mrs. Samuels and Mr. Statham, but also to the hearts of these two individuals. In my judgment, Mrs. Samuels is free to leave the state and travel back to her home, as she has been cleared from charges of murder against Kate Marshall."

Again, Judge Lewis strained to try and make out the outline of Mr. Statham. There was now so much light surrounding him, that the judge shielded his eyes with his right hand. He looked down and glanced quickly through the papers in front of him, hoping when he again looked out into the courtroom, things would be normal.

The judge spoke softly and clearly, "Mr. Statham, would you please step to the bench, Sir?"

Al rose and walked to the front. He felt as though he were being transported. There was a warmth in him and around him that was unexplainable. It was as though he were far removed from the world he had known, and his soul was rejoicing with the voices of an angelic choir, the sound of rushing water, a sense of being suspended and the comforting presence of everything he knew to be wonderful and glorious. This had to be some type of transformation from Almighty God.

Judge Lewis felt an inward confidence he had never experienced, and he knew without a doubt that the Albert Statham who stood before him in this court today was blameless. The misguided man of twenty years earlier was simply "no more." The individual standing before him would be an asset to any community. Only God Almighty above could have rehabilitated this man!

"I can find no fault with the man who stands before me today. Mr. Statham, you are free to go. This hearing is dismissed unless the state determines to pursue other issues."

―

Outside the courthouse Belle started coming back to life. She clung to Les and Clay, and felt life coming back into her being. *Oh, my heavenly Father, how I thank You for carrying all of us through this deep valley. We trusted You to bring about good so that You may be glorified, and Father, You, and You alone, deserve honor. Father, my soul glorifies You.*

A representative from a local television station and another from the local paper stepped up to Al as he walked down the courthouse steps.

"Mr. Statham, could we get your comments, Sir?"

"I guess I would have to sum all of this up in one sentence, and that is the truth sets us free. God above governs man, and unless we walk in the light of Christ there is no truth in us."

"Sir, do you feel that your image and your business will be affected negatively by the publicity of this court hearing today?"

"It is my hope that as I endeavor to place God first in my personal life and business, that He will continue to prosper our company so we can reach out to many and offer another chance. I believe everyone deserves a second chance, and that is the philosophy of our company. Twenty years ago, my choices in life were reckless and my mistakes unforgiveable, but our great God gave me a second chance, and to Him, I give all the credit."

"Sir, do you plan to resign from your business, now?"

"I certainly will, if it would be for the greater good of our people and this community."

"Congratulations, Mr. Statham. We thank you for your time and honesty."

—

John Marshall approached Belle, Les and Clay. He extended his hand first to Belle, then Les, and then embraced his son.

"Dad, thanks for your understanding support during this extremely hurtful time. I know the Lord has carried each of us as only He can. We could not have made it without His faithfulness. I'm flying back home for a few days, and after that will be back to finish up my graduate degree. I will be seeing you regularly then. You have my number, and if you want to talk, call me anytime. I love all of you."

"We love you, too, son," John excused himself and walked down the courthouse steps to depart for home.

Clay stepped back inside the courthouse and located a public telephone.

"Dixie, it is over, we're coming home."

"Oh, Clay, I am so relieved, and I know everyone here will be rejoicing when I share this news. Oh, Darling, I cannot begin to imagine what you've been through. Do be careful. So glad you'll be taking a few days off and flying home with your mom and dad. We all need to relax and enjoy our Lord's bountiful blessings, letting go of the past and throwing out our net to catch a new dream!"

"Well said, my darling. See you soon. I love you with all my heart."

"I love you, too. Bye for now."

As Al awaited Dana and Cole's return home, he found himself more at peace than ever before. *Father, I want to thank You for giving me a Godly fear and humble confidence. Keep me humble, Lord, and devoted to Your service. May every part of my character and conduct serve Your Kingdom purpose. You are the foundation of my hope, my anchor, and there is no treasure so wonderful as Thy grace.*

As he looked up on this very starry night, he saw that his great God had pitched a bright new crescent moon against the majestic night sky. A new moon, a new start, and the greatest gift of all, a redemptive God.

This novel was inspired by the Holy Spirit, and written for the GLORY OF GOD!

J. Laura Chandler
02/07/11

About the Author

Writing *Fingernail Moon* was a five year journey for the author, but the footprints actually began with the memories of her grandfather, Ray Spurgeon Phillips, and the legacy he left of kindness, unselfishness, grace and charity. Ray was remembered for his never having said an unkind word against his fellowman. This thread of Jesus' love and compassion was always obvious to the author through her rich Christian heritage, but until her mother passed away and she was so profoundly beset with grief, she proudly wore the blinders of control and blazed her own course on many a detour from the Truth.

During her mother's final days, Laura witnessed the undeniable courage this little woman exhibited. With each new day, the Lord bestowed new dreams and enthusiasm in the wasted frame of this woman. Thus the death of her mother gave birth to *Fingernail Moon*, as Laura embarked upon the journey of healing.

The author grew up in rural Mississippi along with two brothers, Phillip and Mark. She enjoyed riding horses and training Tennessee Walkers was a big part of her ideal youth. Presently she is retired and lives with her husband in Franklin, TN.

CPSIA information can be obtained at www.ICGtesting.com
Printed in the USA
LVOW060313041011

248975LV00002BA/4/P